CROWN OF EARTH

The Shield, Sword, and Crown:

Shield of Stars
Sword of Waters

The Shield, Sword, and Crown

CROWN OF EARTH

Hilari Bell

Aladdin
New York   London   Toronto   Sydney

ALADDIN
An imprint of Simon & Schuster Children's Publishing Division
1230 Avenue of the Americas, New York, New York 10020
First Aladdin hardcover edition October 2009
Text copyright © 2009 by Hilari Bell
Illustrations copyright © 2009 by Drew Willis
All rights reserved, including the right of reproduction
in whole or in part in any form.
ALADDIN is a trademark of Simon & Schuster, Inc.,
and related logo is a registered trademark of Simon & Schuster, Inc.
For information about special discounts for bulk purchases, please contact
Simon & Schuster Special Sales at 1-866-506-1949 or
business@simonandschuster.com.
The Simon & Schuster Speakers Bureau can bring authors to your live event. For more
information or to book an event contact the Simon & Schuster Speakers Bureau at
1-866-248-3049 or visit our website at www.simonspeakers.com.
Designed by Lucy Ruth Cummins
The text of this book was set in Celestia Antiqua.
Manufactured in the United States of America
2 4 6 8 10 9 7 5 3 1
Library of Congress Cataloging-in-Publication Data
Bell, Hilari.
Crown of earth / Hilari Bell. – 1st ed.
p. cm. — (The shield, sword, and crown ; bk. 3)
Summary: Fifteen-year-old Prince Edoran and fourteen-year-olds
Arisa and Weasel finally realize the true meaning and value of
the symbols of power in Deorthas when the Falcon demands
the sword and shield in exchange for Weasel's life.
ISBN 978-1-4169-0598-1 (hardcover)
[1. Conduct of life—Fiction. 2. Kings, queens, rulers, etc.—Fiction.
3. Signs and symbols—Fiction. 4. Adventure and adventurers—Fiction.
5. Pirates—Fiction. 6. Fantasy.] I. Title.
PZ7.B38894Cro 2009
[Fic]—dc22
2009000912
ISBN 978-1-4169-9694-1 (eBook)

To the volunteers of the Society
of Children's Book
Writers and Illustrators,
past, present, and to come

CHAPTER 1

THE SEVEN OF WATERS

The Seven of Waters: the traveler. A journey begins.

1

They had Weasel.

"I've already sent out troops," said General Diccon. "If they haven't left the city, we'll stop them. If they have, we'll be right on their heels. We'll catch them. We'll probably have them back by morning."

He sounded as if he believed it, but one look at the girl's white face told Edoran that she didn't—and she knew her mother better than any of them.

The crowded office stank of burning lamp oil, sweat, and betrayal. Holis was talking to the stupid peasant boy the Falcon had used as her messenger, trying to persuade him to reveal where the Falcon had taken the kidnapped prince. Or rather, the boy she thought was the kidnapped prince.

They hadn't intended the kidnapping to go so far. Arisa had been certain that hiding the sword and shield would stop her mother's plot. But it had all gone wrong and the Falcon's men had taken Weasel, who was neither their leader's daughter nor the prince. If Diccon's troops didn't catch them . . .

"What do we do if they aren't back by morning?" Edoran demanded. "What if she escapes, with Weasel as a hostage?"

Justice Holis was controlling his expression in front of the Falcon's messenger, but Edoran could see the grimness beneath the mask. "As a hostage . . . I'm afraid Weasel only matters to me. If he's returned alive, unharmed, I might be able to commute her sentence to life imprisonment."

He didn't seem to notice that Arisa flinched, but Edoran did. And judging by his sudden frown, General Diccon saw it too.

"But I can't even promise that," Holis went on, "since I'm not the only one who'll be involved in that decision."

Edoran's heart contracted. He was talking about the horde of shareholders and courtiers who'd swarmed through the palace ever since his father's death. Before his father's death too, but then it hadn't mattered because his father could control them. After the king died, Regent Pettibone had controlled them, and it had mattered a great deal. But there was nothing a five-year-old prince could do about that.

Holis had taken over the regency when the Falcon killed Pettibone, but he didn't yet have the kind of political power Pettibone had wielded. He might never have it, because he didn't want it, and Edoran had almost loved him for that alone. Now he saw the downside to that lack of cutthroat ambition, because the nobles who'd have to approve Holis' judgment on the Falcon wouldn't give a tinker's curse if Weasel lived or died. They'd set terms of surrender that the Falcon would refuse— she'd always struck Edoran as the fight-to-the-death type, and her daughter was the same. She would refuse, and Diccon's troops would attack, and the worthless clerk who'd allowed himself to be kidnapped in Edoran's stead would be the first to die.

"No." It came out sounding remarkably firm, considering that his hands were clammy and his heart was pounding. "I'm involved in that decision. In fact, I'm going to make it."

"Your Highness." Holis looked pained. "The shareholders—"

"Can rot!" Edoran rose to his feet. "General Diccon, you have till tomorrow's dawn to capture the Falcon and return her and her hostage to the palace. If they aren't here by sunrise, you will meet me in the courtyard with a troop of sufficient strength to guarantee my safety. Then we'll go after the Falcon, and when we find her I will personally oversee the negotiations for her surrender. Is that clear?"

The general looked appalled at the mere prospect. "Yes, Your Highness, but—"

"I command this." If he stayed, if he let them argue, they would win. Edoran turned and walked out. Maybe the deliberate stride that was all his wobbling knees could manage would be mistaken for confidence, or authority, or something. But he had to get out. He had to get out of that hot little room where his best friend was being condemned to death out of political necessity.

Political necessity resulting in death was nothing new to Edoran—though before Weasel came, when he'd had no friends, it hadn't seemed as important as it did now.

Edoran stalked away, ignoring the guard who stood outside the office door—who must have failed to close that door after his prince, for General Diccon's voice echoed into the corridor. "Well, I'll be hanged. The little runt sounded like a king!"

Heat flooded Edoran's face, but he kept walking. Pretending that he didn't hear the whispers, didn't know what people thought of him, was even more familiar than the fear that his own murder might suddenly become politically necessary.

Only four months ago the speech he'd just made would have signed his death warrant.

As long as you're of use to me, the old regent's voice murmured in his memory.

But after Holis had taken the regency from Pettibone, that fear had slowly subsided. Holis' political power was weak enough that he couldn't rule Deorthas unless he did so in Edoran's name. And . . . he really didn't seem like the murdering type. He kept telling Edoran that he was a prince—maybe he meant it. But whether he meant it or not, he had to keep up the pretense of Edoran's authority or his own would fail.

If I stand firm, if I insist, they have to do it.

If they didn't, if he caved in, then Weasel might die.

Edoran quickened his pace through the maze of hallways, ignoring both the courtiers' startled looks and the quaking in his guts.

His new valet must have heard something; he'd opened the gilded doors of the prince's suite and was peering out, waiting for him.

"I need you to go to the stable," Edoran told him curtly. "Inform the grooms that I'll need Ginger, saddled and ready, in the courtyard at dawn tomorrow. And Rudolphus, too. I may need a remount if I'm going to keep up."

The valet gawked at him. Edoran hadn't yet figured out who he was spying for, and at this moment he didn't care.

"Now!"

"Ah, of course, Your Highness. Might I inquire—"

"No," said Edoran. "I gave you an order. Obey it."

The valet departed, and Edoran just made it to the privy before vomiting up the remains of his early dinner. Stress had always affected his stomach, but there wasn't much to come up. It was almost midnight now. Swapping costumes, helping Arisa hide the sword and shield from her mother's men, interrogating that worthless boy—it had all taken far too long. He and Arisa had spent more than an hour locked in a closet!

He winced at the memory of her weeping. She was the craziest person he'd ever known, but she loved her mother, and Weasel was as much her friend as he was Edoran's. More.

Some part of Edoran had wanted to hate her for taking that extra share of Weasel's attention, but even he could see that wouldn't be fair. And in her strange, half-wild way, she'd tried to help him. Was there any way he could get the Falcon out of this when he saved Weasel?

He'd be willing to try, for Arisa's sake. The Falcon had wanted to take over Deorthas, but it sometimes seemed to Edoran that everyone he knew was trying to take over Deorthas, and she hadn't threatened to kill him or anyone else . . . so far.

If she killed Weasel, all bets were off. But that wouldn't happen. Edoran wouldn't let it happen, even if he had to throw screaming fits to force them to listen.

By the time his valet returned, he'd stripped off Weasel's costume, donned his riding clothes, retrieved the smallest bag he could find from the little room where his clothes were stored, and started packing. He'd been in that room only a couple of times in his life, though its door opened off his own bedroom; it took him almost five minutes to locate the cupboard that held the luggage.

"I have conveyed your orders to the grooms," his valet announced. "Ah, might I assist you with that?"

"Please," said Edoran, gratefully abandoning his attempt to fold a shirt. "I'll be traveling rough. I don't know for how long. Just riding clothes. Nothing fancy."

"Packing for at least a week? Indeed." The valet nodded, went into Edoran's closet, and came out with one of the large trunks he'd already rejected.

"Not that," said Edoran. "I'll be traveling on horseback, with an army troop."

He wasn't about to allow General Diccon to refuse to take him because he had too much luggage.

"Very good, Your Highness," said his valet. "Your luggage can go in the carriage."

"We'll be traveling fast," Edoran repeated, trying not to snap at the man. "There won't be any carriage."

"But there must be, if Your Highness is with them," said his valet serenely. "How else could I, and your cook, and the groom accompany you? How else could your foodstuffs be carried?" He smiled indulgently at Edoran's foolishness.

"I won't be taking any servants," said Edoran, through gritted teeth. "I'll eat whatever the soldiers eat. We have to travel fast!"

"Of course, Your Highness." The valet folded an embroidered

vest neatly into the trunk. "Do you know if you'll be stopping at inns? Or will you stay at the shareholders' manors?"

Edoran finally dismissed the man, coming close to the screaming fit he'd planned to use only as a last resort. He managed to cram one pair of clean britches and several shirts into a small bag, along with his underclothes and the toiletries he'd need to keep himself clean. He could find someone to wash and press them after he'd caught up with Weasel.

Perhaps he should have worn the burglar costume Weasel had given him—it was both comfortable and practical—but his own riding clothes felt more . . . familiar. It had been Arisa's idea to disguise herself in Edoran's costume, to be kidnapped in his place, since her mother's men would never dare harm her—but she'd been too big for Edoran's clothes. They'd fit Weasel perfectly, even though both he and Arisa were only a year younger than Edoran's fifteen.

Soon he was ready to leave, but dawn was still hours off and his eyelids were beginning to droop. For some reason he always woke up at sunrise, but he needed to be down in the courtyard when the sun was coming up, not fumbling into his clothes and splashing water on his face. He didn't want to summon his valet and have the man try to pack for him again. Was there any servant he could trust to wake him before dawn?

No. There was no one he could trust.

In the end Edoran spent the rest of the night, fully clothed, in a chair in his sitting room, dozing off and then waking when his stiff muscles protested. It was more than an hour before sunrise when he gave up on sleep and picked up his pack and the fur-lined cloak he'd selected for traveling in late winter. The rains that had drenched the city for the past few weeks might have abated but it was still cold, and if they traveled away from the coast there might be snow. It wouldn't fit in his satchel, but it could be tied on the back of his saddle if he grew too warm. If he'd forgotten anything, he could borrow it from some trooper once they were on the road.

Edoran's heart lightened as he let himself out of his rooms and crept down the long corridors to the main doors. The palace was silent. Not even the servants who cleaned the hearths and brought hot water were stirring yet. The palace had seemed large to him as a child, but this was the first time he'd encountered it when it was . . . empty.

He felt like a character in some fable, as if when he reached the courtyard he'd find it overgrown with vines, signifying that a hundred years had passed, or that all the servants had been turned into mice while he slept in that uncomfortable chair. But when he opened the doors, only the normal darkness of night transformed the familiar park and garden.

An hour and fifteen minutes till dawn. He knew it without even glancing at the sky, for he always knew when the sun would rise and set.

The troop captains were probably waking their men right now, and they'd be packing—unless they'd done that last night? Edoran had never dealt with even the palace guards, much less the common army soldiers. That would change soon, for General

Diccon would bring them here at dawn. No matter what he might think of his prince's command, he had to obey it.

The Falcon had believed that Diccon was loyal to Prince Edoran. Edoran could have told her that the general was loyal to Deorthas, and couldn't have cared less about Edoran himself.

The grooms would be bringing his horses soon too. Ginger, chosen for her easy paces, and Rudolphus, for his stamina. If the grooms were late . . . could Edoran saddle a horse himself? He never had, and when he'd watched it looked pretty complicated. But surely the stable roused early. They had his orders. The horses would arrive.

The sky had gone from black to slate gray. They were probably saddling his horses right now. And the troops would be readying their own horses, for their prince had given them an order and he hadn't backed down or caved in. So they had to obey.

The sky grew brighter. Birds began to sing in the trees of the park. Edoran could hear muffled sounds from the palace, where the lower servants had started working.

But it wasn't dawn yet. The horses and the troops he'd ordered weren't late. Not quite. Even if they were late, they had to obey his direct command. He was the prince! As long as he held firm, what else could they do?

The sun rose, light flooding the courtyard. Sometimes men were late. Especially starting a journey that might last for an unknown amount of time, at sunrise. They were probably in the midst of frantic preparations, the officers shouting that they were keeping Prince Edoran waiting, that if they didn't get a move on, when he turned twenty-two and became king he'd fire the lazy lot of them. He would, if they didn't get here soon. They had to come soon. What else could they do?

The sun rose higher. No one came into the courtyard. No frantic grooms, hurrying up with his horses. No troops. No general, apologizing for the delay. Edoran couldn't even see any servants peering through the windows, though he'd bet they were there, enjoying his humiliation. He'd fire them, too, when he became king, and have Diccon hanged! Or at least thrown in jail.

He imagined the weeping grooms walking through the front gate, carrying bundles that held all their worldly goods. Diccon, begging his king for mercy.

Weasel, who'd started his life as a pickpocket, had always been terrified of going to jail. . . .

How could he save Weasel? How could he do anything, if they simply ignored his orders? If they all behaved as if he'd never given any orders? And they were doubtless doing it at Justice Holis' command. When he turned twenty-two, he'd have Holis hanged as well!

But for now he was powerless. He'd have to slink back into the palace and pretend . . . that he hadn't been serious? That he really was the incompetent joke everyone thought he was?

He couldn't even saddle his own horse! How could he expect to save Weasel when . . .

Weasel and Arisa had walked almost half the length of Deorthas last fall, when Weasel had rescued Justice Holis. At least Edoran could walk.

And in the eyes of the common folk of Deorthas he *was* the prince. If he could find the Falcon himself, if he could be there when the negotiations for her surrender took place . . . Holis couldn't ignore orders that Edoran gave in public without undermining his own authority, because his authority rested on Edoran's.

He'd watched Pettibone playing that game long enough to know the rules. And if Holis was strong enough to stand up to him in public, Edoran would make it crystal clear to every shareholder who was part of those negotiations that if Weasel died they would die too, on the day of his twenty-second birthday. They'd have to believe that he meant it, because it was true.

The trick would be to find the Falcon, to make contact with her, without getting captured himself. If she had Edoran in her hands, she'd have no reason to care about Weasel's fate—and he wasn't crazy enough to want another homicidal regent, either. But that was a problem for the future.

In order to negotiate with the Falcon, or to have any influence when someone else did, Edoran had to be there, physically on the spot. Ready to convince people that he would one day have the power, and the will, to hang them if they let him down.

It was good that they hadn't brought his horses. If he'd tried to ride out the gates, the guards might have stopped him. As it was . . . Weasel himself had shown both Arisa and Edoran the places where you could climb over the palace wall. It felt right to use them.

Prince Edoran picked up his satchel and walked across the lawns, into the trees of the park.

CHAPTER 2

THE FIVE OF FIRES

*The Five of Fires: the thief. Sudden loss of wealth
from any cause. May indicate blighted crops
or a poor harvest.*

2

He found the place where the stones were crumbling with little difficulty, and climbed it with only a little more. He'd already done it several times at night, and it proved easier in the daylight.

Peering over the top, waiting for a moment when the street was clear of carts and pedestrians, Edoran remembered that his father had written about this wall in his journal. What had he said? A joke even to keep burglars out, much less an army. His father had been interested in fortifications. He'd been looking into the possibility of building a wall between Deorthas and the Isolian Duchies, which sometimes looked toward Deorthas with conquest in mind, but the king had died before the engineers at the university had even started to study the project.

Edoran sometimes wondered if he'd be able to read at all if it wasn't for his father's journals. The tutors Pettibone hired had been paid to keep the prince from learning anything that might someday make him dangerous—or even look like less of an idiot.

But once he'd realized that some part of his father lived on in those journals, Edoran had to read them. So he'd taught himself, sounding out the words, sneaking into the schoolroom to use the big dictionary when his tutors were gone.

He'd sometimes felt that his father was trying to teach him the things he'd need in order to survive and become king—though as he grew older, Edoran knew that had to be wishful thinking. Still, he could see this wall through his father's eyes as the pitiful structure it was—even if the drop to the cobbles jarred his bones when the traffic finally cleared.

He'd walked six blocks, being jostled by servants and craftsmen on their way to work, before he realized that he didn't even know what direction the Falcon had gone when she'd taken Weasel and fled.

This stopped him in his tracks for several seconds, but the city only had three main gates. Even if the guards there didn't remember her departure, they'd certainly have noticed the troop that Diccon had sent in pursuit.

But which gate? There was no way to know, but the palace was closer to the west gate, so he decided to try it first.

He set off again at a brisk walk, and if he didn't enjoy being jostled by all and sundry, he did enjoy the fact that no one paid any attention to him.

Back at the palace they'd probably assume he'd gone into the park to sulk. It would be hours before anyone went to look for him, and still more hours, maybe a full day, before they realized he'd left the palace grounds.

If the Falcon, or her men, were going to kill Weasel when they first discovered the switch, there was no way anyone could reach them in time to prevent it. There was no reason for Edoran to feel like he ought to be running through the crowded streets. He did look back once or twice, but no one was pursuing him. He even took a moment, when he found himself growing warm despite the cool morning, to wrap his cloak into a bundle and strap it to the bottom of his satchel. It was heavier to carry than he'd thought.

By the time he reached the west gate, he'd begun to believe he'd actually escaped. And the less he stood out in anyone's memory, the longer it would take Justice Holis and the general to find his trail. Would simply asking the gate guard if a troop had passed through fix Edoran in their memory?

Weasel, no doubt, would engage them in casual conversation and coax them around to the topic so skillfully that they'd answer his question without even realizing that was what he wanted. But how did one go about that?

Edoran slowed his pace, studying the guards. There were two of them, one Edoran could see through the window of the tower where the records were kept, and another standing outside the gate tower with his back against the wall, keeping an eye on the passersby. He had no duty to interfere with people going in and out of the city, unless for some reason they seemed to pose a threat. For all they wore the green and white uniform of the city guard, they carried neither pistol nor sword. Their job was more that of accountants, recording the contents of the carts that went in and out for Deorthas' tax officials, than of real guards.

An accountant wasn't going to be as suspicious as a real guard. Right?

Edoran strolled up to the tower, trying to make his approach look casual. "Good morning. I hear you had some excitement here last night."

The guard who stood by the tower wall was a thin man with a frowning face. "What are you talking about?"

"I heard a big troop went through last night, chasing after someone. Or something."

"Where'd you hear that?" the guard demanded. Quite rudely, Edoran thought. How much knowledge would a common citizen have? Surely if troops went galloping through the city they might gossip about it.

"It's just being talked about." He gestured vaguely to the shops lining the street behind him. "Around."

"And why do you want to know?" the thin guard asked.

The other guard came to the window, his curious gaze on Edoran.

"What goes in and out of this gate is Prince Edoran's business," the thin guard finished, "and his alone."

"Exactly. I mean, that's a very proper attitude, but I'm sure the prince wouldn't care if you just confirmed that a troop had passed. Or not. We heard . . . My father heard that they were chasing after some of those pirates who've been raiding the coastal villages. He's got some cargo he wants to ship, and he was hoping it would soon be safe to do so. If they're about to catch the pirates, I mean," he finished with some relief.

It sounded plausible to Edoran, but the guard's frown deepened. The guard inside the tower looked interested.

"There was nothing about a troop in the night shift's records," he told the prince. "You say they found some of those pirates? Here in the city?"

"That's what my father heard," said Edoran. "But you know how gossip is. He was hoping your records might confirm it. Or at least that a troop had passed."

"The records of the city guard are confidential," the first guard snapped, speaking to both Edoran and his colleague. "And you should know better than to reveal them to every passing scamp! He might—"

"Why not?" the guard in the tower demanded. "If a troop had passed, half the street would know about it, and there's no harm in confirming something everyone already knows, now is there?"

Edoran crept away under cover of their argument. These guards would certainly remember him if anyone asked—but it wouldn't be hard for Holis to deduce that he'd gone after Weasel, anyway. He'd learned what he needed to know—the Falcon's men hadn't set out to the west.

He spent the walk to the north gate preparing his story. His father was a spice merchant, a cargo pirates particularly liked to seize because it was both small and valuable. He needed to ship it soon, and he'd rather send it by sea if he could be certain it would be safe. Edoran was the youngest of three sons.

He marched up to the next gate tower with some confidence, even though both guards were sitting on a bench outside, holding mugs of something that steamed in the crisp air.

"I heard a rumor that a big troop went through this gate last night. Chasing some of those pirates that have been raiding ashore." He was probably starting that rumor himself, Edoran realized. He hoped no harm would come of it.

One of the guards raised his brows. "Not that I know of," he said. "Night shift say anything to you about a troop, Jas?"

"There wasn't nothing in the notes," Jas said. "And they'd have mentioned it."

The first guard turned back to Edoran. "Sorry, lad. They didn't pass through here."

"Thank you," said Edoran. He waited a moment, in case they wanted to ask some question that would let him use the story he'd prepared, but the guard only nodded in dismissal, so he left.

It felt odd to be turned away so casually. They hadn't even risen to their feet to address him. Of course, there was no reason they should. It just felt . . . odd.

Approaching the third gate, Edoran thought he was ready for anything.

"Pirates, you say?" This guard was standing in the shade of the wall, warming his hands over a brazier. "Well, I pray to the One God they get 'em."

"They went out this gate?" Edoran asked, hardly daring to believe it.

"Right around midnight, according to what the night shift said. And better them than us," the guard added. "Galloping around in the dark is just asking for a broken neck. Though if they could catch some of those murdering scum, it might be worth the risk."

He spat onto the cobbles, and Edoran stepped back a pace, though the spittle had come nowhere near his boots. "I thank you."

He walked through the east gate without further ado. He was on Weasel's trail! Well, he was on the trail of the men who were on Weasel's trail, but that should amount to the same thing. And it would be far easier to follow a mounted troop through the countryside than a group of brigands who were trying to avoid people's attention. Unless the troop lost its quarry, this was surely the wiser choice.

It proved easy enough throughout that morning, for both the farmer who was raking up some brown viney things, and the girl selling hot pastries to coach passengers in the first village Edoran went through, confirmed that the troop had passed that way. Indeed, the girl had been awakened when they galloped down the village's main street in the middle of the night, and she would have told Edoran about it at length if a coach hadn't pulled up and distracted her.

It passed Edoran on the road a few minutes later, and he barely leaped aside in time to keep from being splattered by the mud from its wheels.

The footpath beside the road was mostly dry, but the road wasn't. Still, the day was bright despite the chill. Birds chirped and twittered in the patches of scrub between the plowed fields, and hopped about looking for seeds in the open places. And Edoran thought he was doing very well, for someone who had never left the city without an escort.

His weather sense was warning him that a medium-heavy rain would start shortly after darkness fell and continue for about two hours before tapering off. Edoran remembered how the first pirate raid had felt: the black sickness in his gut; the slices of cold through his lungs that he somehow knew for steel swords and the thick flow of blood . . . without having any idea who was dying by those swords, or where, or why. What use was that to anyone?

At least his awareness of the storm that was currently spilling its rain into the sea held no pain or death—and was useful besides, for he knew he'd have all day to get to the shelter of some inn.

And speaking of an inn, he was getting hungry! But it took another full hour of walking before he reached the next village—this one almost large enough to be considered a small town. Edoran had a vague memory of stopping here for a luncheon once, when he'd been out with a party of riders. . . . Yes, there it was. The Hunting Hound wasn't large, only a single taproom with no private parlors, but its diamond-paned windows glowed with cleanliness. Its walls were of brick and its roof of stone, not the thatch that poorer inns still sometimes used in the country. If he remembered correctly, the food had been good.

They were doing a brisk business, Edoran noted as he opened the door. Possibly because of the roasting ham, the scent of which was strong enough to make his mouth water. He went in and seated himself at one of the few empty tables, stashing his cloak and satchel beneath it, and waited for the serving girl to bustle over to him.

She didn't. Of course, like the tower guards that morning, she didn't know he was the prince. There was no reason, as far as she knew, why she shouldn't first serve the red-faced man in the puce coat. And then the thin man with ink-stained fingers. But when she brought more tea for an older woman in a threadbare gown, Edoran began to fume. And it didn't appease him that she hustled over to his table next—he was hungry!

"Good day, young goodman," she said cheerfully, as if she hadn't kept him waiting. "We've a mushroom-and-potato soup in the pot, and—"

"I'll have some of that ham," Edoran told her, having made up his mind while he waited. "And beans amandine, and rolls with honey butter. And an apple . . . no, apricot tarts for dessert. If you please," he added politely, since she had no way of knowing he was the prince.

The girl's mouth opened, then closed. She looked Edoran over, paying particular attention to his clothing and boots, though why she'd care about them he had no idea.

"We've none of that made up, young sir," she told him. "Not even the ham, for it's on the spit for dinner and won't be done till then."

"You could cut a piece off the outside and cook it quickly, couldn't you?" Edoran asked. "And prepare the other things quickly as well?" Whatever he asked for appeared from the palace kitchen in very short order.

"We could make it up," the girl admitted. "All but the apricot tarts, for we've no apricot preserves. But if we rushed it, an apple tart might be ready close to the end of your meal. Thing is—"

"Then the apple tart will be fine," Edoran told her graciously.

"The thing is, young sir, making all that up will cost you extra. A lot extra." The girl's gaze returned to his muddy boots, and her wary voice grew firmer. "Excuse me if it seems rude, but you've not been here before. I'll have to see that you can pay before I take your order to the kitchen."

Pay? He hadn't thought . . . He'd taken the purse that he used for tipping strange servants and put it in his pocket, as he always did when he planned to leave the palace, but he had no idea how much was in it. His old valet had kept it stocked with small coins, but Edoran didn't know if the new man had refilled it. He also had no idea how much the meal he'd just ordered would cost. The girl's foot was beginning to tap impatiently, though she held the polite expression on her face. And there was only one way to find out.

Edoran pulled out his purse and tipped the contents onto the table. There were fewer coins than usual, so the new man probably hadn't refilled it; nothing but a few copper flames, brass droplets, and mostly tin nothings—as were appropriate for tipping servants for small errands. Like bringing food. So perhaps . . .

"Is this enough for my meal?" Edoran asked hopefully.

"Not even close." The girl's polite expression had vanished. "Not even enough for soup and bread, which is the cheapest meal the Hunting Hound serves. The Black Pig might have something you could afford, but if you don't mind, we need this table for customers who can pay."

Edoran's face was hot, and he knew he was blushing furiously as he gathered up his cloak and satchel and departed. Curse the girl, she didn't have to sneer like that. How could he have known he couldn't afford a meal? He'd never had to pay for one before.

On the rare occasions he'd traveled, his servants had taken care of things like that.

And more important than his embarrassment, he was still hungry! He continued down the street to the Black Pig, but one look at its dilapidated thatch and peeling paint warned him, and one whiff of the stale stench drifting from the taproom told Edoran that he couldn't eat there.

He finally managed to purchase a day-old loaf from a baker and some cheese from a village goodwife the baker had recommended. This took slightly more than half of his small stock of coins, but it wasn't too bad a meal. An apple would have improved it, but the goodwife had told him what an apple would cost, out of season now, as all fruits were, and he couldn't afford it. He couldn't really afford the dented tin water flask the goodwife had sold him, but that was something he had to have.

At least the remainder of the bread and cheese would serve for his dinner, Edoran reflected as he tramped on down the road. And perhaps a bit of breakfast tomorrow. He would soon have to work for his meals and a place to sleep, just as Weasel and Arisa had done on their adventures. He'd never worked before, but everyone did it—how hard could it be?

The misunderstanding at the inn had been humiliating, but no harm had come from it. He could still rescue Weasel. But his cheerful mood had been broken, and things that hadn't bothered him in the morning, such as the puddles he was forced to skirt, annoyed him now.

There was more traffic on the road in the afternoon, some of it moving fast enough that Edoran had to leap aside to avoid the splashing mud, and his growing awareness of the storm reminded him of the need for shelter.

Unfortunately, by the time dusk began to gather he was still some distance from the nearest town, or even any villages, as far as he could tell. He had several more hours before the rain would start, but real cold was arriving as the sun set, and he'd hardly slept at all last night. Even if he donned his cloak, navigating the rough path in the darkness held no appeal.

Could he stop at a farm and ask for a room for the night? They would doubtless want him to pay, and he had no idea how much. He could face the necessity of working at some simple chore to pay for his meals and lodging tomorrow, but he was too tired to do it tonight. Yet what other choice . . .

The shed was some distance off the road, and it looked almost as dilapidated as the Black Pig. But Weasel had said that he and Arisa once waited out a storm in a hay shed, and that the roof had been sound. It hadn't sounded too uncomfortable, and surely no one would expect him to pay to sleep in a shed.

Edoran made up his mind and left the path, climbing through the split rails of the fence that stood between him and rest, and shelter. Surely his cloak would keep him warm, especially with a bit of hay piled atop it.

The empty field had looked fairly level from the road, but it wasn't. Crossing it splashed mud onto any patch of Edoran's boots that hadn't been muddy before, but he was now too tired to care. The door creaked as it opened, but the faint, familiar scent of

horses reached out to him, and he was suddenly glad that the road had emptied of traffic as the sun set, glad that he hadn't reached an inn. He'd had enough of people for—

A hard hand between his shoulder blades shoved him forward, to fall to his hands and knees on the dusty floor.

He heard boot steps on the hollow wood, and the creak of the door closing behind them. Trying to fight down panic, he rose to his feet and turned to face them. If these were farmhands, indignant at his trespass . . .

They weren't. One look at their hard faces would have told Edoran that, even without the knives in their hands.

There were four of them, more than he could possibly fight. A moment ago he would have sworn he couldn't have run, but now he knew that terror would have sent him flying down the road . . . had he been on the road. Trapped in this dusty shed, with the last of the daylight leaking through the cracks in its walls, he could neither fight nor flee.

He liked to think he had too much pride to beg, so he tried to keep his voice from quivering. "If it's my purse you're after, I'm afraid you've come to the wrong place. I've hardly any money, but what there is . . ." He pulled his thin purse from his pocket and cast it to the floor at their feet. "I won't say you're welcome to it, but I can't prevent you from taking it, so you might as well."

And then go.

The shortest of the four men laughed. "Well played, lad. But we don't want that purse. We want your real one."

Edoran blinked. "That is my real purse."

"The other purse, then. The one with your money in it."

Were they mad? "That is the purse. With my money in it."

The short bandit sighed. "It may save some time if I tell you that I was . . . that we heard what happened in the Hunting Hound."

He'd been in the Hunting Hound, which might help the town guard find him if Edoran survived to report this conversation. But . . .

"What does that have to do with anything? I didn't even eat there."

"Exactly. I mean, why would you go and order a big meal, all special, if you couldn't pay for it? We're not fools, boy. Anyone whose purse is so rich that he'd rather walk out hungry than show it in public, well, he's worth following. And you ought t' learn to look behind you once in a while. Never followed anyone so easy. And since you made it so easy on us, if you'll just hand over that purse you didn't care to show off in the Hound, why, we'll take it and be on our way and no harm done to you. You know you can't fight us, so you might as well hand it over."

Edoran did know it. If he'd had such a purse, he would have been cowardly enough to do just that. Could you be a coward for something you wanted to do, but couldn't?

Heart sinking, his stomach in knots, Edoran threw his satchel aside, and when their eyes followed it he leaped for the door.

He wasn't surprised when hard hands caught his collar and one arm. This time they slammed him facedown onto the floor, hard enough that several moments passed before his mind cleared.

"That wasn't smart, boy," the short bandit, who seemed to be the leader, told him. He'd already scooped up Edoran's satchel and was pulling out shirts and underclothes.

"I haven't got another purse," Edoran protested.

The short bandit sighed again. None of the others said a word. Afraid something about their voices would allow him to identify them? But Edoran had already seen their faces.

The leader inspected Edoran's satchel and then pulled out his knife. The prince flinched, and the hands that held him down tightened. But the bandit only sliced open the lining and seams of his satchel—in moments it lay in shreds on the floor.

The leader picked up the cloak he'd cast aside. It was too dark to make out his expression now, but Edoran saw him hesitate; then he sheathed his knife.

He spent several minutes running his hands over the hems and collar, then the whole length of the finely woven wool, then through the soft fur of the lining.

"Just cut it up!" one of the men holding Edoran snapped, proving that they could speak. And also that they didn't care if some accent gave Edoran a clue where he might find them, which was probably a bad sign.

"It's valuable, dolt," the leader replied. "If there were coins sewn in we could feel 'em. But there aren't."

"I told you, the small purse is all the money I have." Edoran heard the plea creeping into his voice and hated it—though he would have begged for mercy if he thought it would work.

"Ah, but I saw your little purse dumped out in the Hound," the bandit said. "There's nothing in there worth stealing. And we've followed you a long way this afternoon."

He drew his knife.

Edoran scrabbled frantically on the dirty floor, trying to rise, to flee, to break the grip that held him down. It earned him a kick in the ribs that made him gasp. When the pain had lessened enough for him to breathe again, the short bandit was ripping up his coat with the knife.

They cut it off his body and sliced it to shreds. They cut the collar off his shirt and slit the waist and knee bands of his britches, cuffing and punching him if he tried to fight.

Then they shoved him face-first onto the floor once more and shredded the clothes that had been pulled from his pack.

"What about the heels of his boots?" one of them demanded.

"No room there to hide enough coin to bother with," the leader said. "Nor under the soles, neither." Though he took his knife and pried the inner soles out of Edoran's boots anyway.

It was dark in the shed now, but Edoran could see when the man turned toward him, slapping the knife blade thoughtfully into his palm.

"I told you I hadn't any money." This time he couldn't keep his voice from shaking.

"Maybe he hid it somewhere in the shed," one of them suggested.

The leader snorted. "He didn't have time for that. We followed him right through the door, remember? But maybe . . . maybe he swallowed it."

Edoran's blood ran cold. He tried to protest, to deny it, but even his voice was paralyzed with horror.

"But if it was in his belly, he wouldn't have ordered that luncheon before thinking twice about showing his coin," the bandit went on. "And as for doing it later, he didn't know we were following him, so he'd no need. Besides, it's harder to swallow a coin than you might think. I tried it once and cursed near choked to death."

He paused again and Edoran waited, his heart hammering against the rough wood of the floor.

"So I'm inclined to believe he's telling the truth," the bandit finished. "And he really has no more coin than this."

He went over to the corner, picked up Edoran's purse, and put it in his pocket.

"You mean we wasted this whole afternoon for nothing?" another of the bandits snarled.

"Not for nothing," the short man said. "This cloak'll be worth a fair bit of silver, in a town big enough to fence it. Worth gold if we could sell it honest, but that's neither here nor there."

The hard hands holding Edoran to the floor relaxed a bit, and he stifled a sob of relief. They were going to go. They were going to go, and not rip open his stomach with that big knife before they departed.

The short man came over to where Edoran lay and stared down at him. "Let this be a lesson to you, lad," he said. "Don't go ordering up things you can't pay for."

Edoran saw the boot swing toward his face, but he was held down too securely to do anything about it.

He didn't lose consciousness, exactly. He could feel the hands releasing their pressure on his back. He heard the small sounds as the four men left the shed and closed the door behind them. But he couldn't move, or even open his eyes, for several minutes after they'd gone. Maybe more than minutes, for by the time he opened his eyes again the moon had risen.

His dark-adapted eyes made out more than he'd expected, and when he crawled to the door and opened it he could see even more. There was nothing left of his satchel but scraps, and the clothing he'd packed was no better. He'd had to grab his britches and hold them up, or they'd have fallen off before he reached the door.

The bread and cheese had been trampled into crumbs, and at some point, without his noticing, someone had emptied his water flask. That discovery almost made him weep, for he was horribly thirsty. And dirty, and the whole left side of his face throbbed, along with his aching ribs and assorted lesser bruises.

He was afraid to leave, because they might be waiting for him. He was afraid to stay for fear they might change their minds and come back. He could freeze to death without his cloak; this shed held only harness and farm tools, no friendly hay to warm and hide him.

More than anything, Edoran wanted to be back in his own bed, in his own suite, with servants who would bring him hot drinks and salve for his bruises, whether they liked him or not.

He could go back. Assuming he didn't freeze, he had only to reach the road tomorrow morning. Once the traffic started up, the first carriage that came past would return him to the palace. Edoran himself could reward them for it, if Holis didn't.

But if he did that, when the negotiations for the Falcon's surrender began, Weasel might die.

He might be dead already.

Edoran lowered his aching body to the floor and curled up, trying to keep warm.

Weasel might be dead, but he probably wasn't, and Edoran continuing to follow him was the best chance of survival Weasel had. He couldn't quit. He wouldn't quit!

But how could he go on, with no food, no money, no clothes . . . ?

It was then that he felt it, a faint . . . warmth at the edge of his consciousness. But he knew that warmth meant safety, help, and ease for his painful bruises. It wasn't far off, whatever it was. He only had to get there, and then he could rest.

It hurt his ribs to pull on his boots, but at least his boots were more or less intact. His head throbbed when he struggled to his feet and went back to the door.

The waxing moon cast shadows into the nearby scrub, but he didn't see any lurking bandits. And if he stayed there, if he didn't get help, he'd probably run out of will and be ready to give up his quest by morning.

Edoran drew a steadying breath of the cold air and set off in search of the shelter he sensed, somewhere in the darkness.

CHAPTER 3

THE TWO OF FIRES

The Two of Fires: jealousy.
Coveting something you haven't earned.

3

The first thing Edoran saw, through the bare branches, was the flickering light of a fire. His sensing had led him down the farmer's path and over another rough field, or possibly two, to a shallow ravine filled with trees.

Edoran stopped, suddenly wary. His strange instincts, which he'd learned to trust, told him this fire spelled safety and aid, but the events of the day made him cautious. Even if his peculiar gift was right, if anyone around that fire recognized him they might well offer him shelter and aid . . . and send him straight back to the palace in the morning. He needed to see who they were before he revealed himself.

Moving as quietly as he could, keeping the thickest under-brush between him and the light, Edoran crept forward. The clearing was so tiny that no one could have found it if they hadn't known it was there, and the trickle of water that cut a trough on its far side was too small to call a stream. It reminded Edoran of his thirst—he'd drink even dirty water, if he had no other choice.

But not if it meant falling into the hands of General Diccon's soldiers. Though this clearing was too small to hold a guard troop. In fact . . . He crept nearer, until he could see the whole of the open space—there was no one there. But someone had built that fire, and thrown a blanket over a pile of gear that lay off to one side. If they weren't there, then where—

He was already starting to turn when the shove sent him toppling onto the dry grass. He scrambled to his feet—this time he would fight, by the One God! But before he even located his opponent, a familiar voice exclaimed, "You! What are you doing here?"

A familiar female voice. Arisa emerged from the shadows as if the forest itself had spawned her. How had she sneaked up through all that dry brush without him hearing her? He really had to learn to look behind him. But what in the world . . .

"What are *you* doing here?" Edoran demanded. "I thought you—" Then he caught sight of the curve under the blanket she'd cast over her gear, and poking out from under its folds, the tip of a pommel. Most people wouldn't have recognized them, but Edoran had spent the better portion of the disaster last night trying to hide them from her mother's men.

"You didn't!"

Arisa went to the blanket and picked it up, revealing the sword and shield. "Clearly, I did. Wrap yourself up." She pitched the blanket to Edoran. "You're shivering."

"Are you stark staring mad?" Edoran wrapped the blanket around himself and sat beside the fire. Its warmth dispelled the terrors of the night. "Do you have any water?" he added.

She pulled a flask from her pack and handed it to him. "Do you believe the sword and shield are more important than Weasel's life?"

"No," he admitted. "But . . . You stole them? You just . . . stole them?" The cool water tasted faintly of the metal of her flask, and trickling down his parched throat, it was the most wonderful thing he'd ever tasted.

"Yes," she said simply. "What happened to your face?"

"I can't believe you did that," Edoran muttered. It had taken some nerve to run away from the palace himself. To steal the most precious artifacts in the kingdom, the symbols that, to most of the country folk of Deorthas, mattered almost as much as the king himself . . . He wouldn't have dared. And he was, technically, their owner. Arisa was the daughter of a rebel and traitor, who had just fled after trying to kidnap the prince.

Edoran had to take another swallow of water before he could summon his voice. "They'll hang you. They'll decide that you were working with the Falcon all along and hang you right beside her. You really are out of your mind."

Arisa shrugged. "It looks to me like you've got no room to criticize." Her gaze traveled over him, taking in the bruises, the tattered clothing. "Got yourself robbed, did you?"

If there'd been any sympathy in her voice, Edoran probably would have burst into tears. As it was, he managed to keep his voice almost calm as he told the tale of his adventures. She soaked a kerchief in the stream to make a cold compress for his face and gave him a bit of food from her pack—bread and cheese, very like the stuff he'd lost, though she'd purchased some raisins to go with it. She shook her head in astonishment when he was done.

"And you call me crazy."

"I suppose we're both a little crazy," Edoran admitted. "But we also have . . . how to put this . . . a common cause? We both want to get Weasel back alive. You were going to trade your mother the sword and shield for him, weren't you?"

The girl nodded slowly. "They'd make a much more valuable hostage than Weasel would. Maybe valuable enough that she could trade them for safe passage out of Deorthas. It's not only Weasel I'm trying to save, you know."

"I have no problem with that," said Edoran promptly. "All she's done is plot to seize the throne, and sooner or later everyone does that. It's not like she's killed anyone."

Yet. That they knew of. He pulled the blanket closer. He refused to believe that. Weasel was alive. He had to be.

"She probably killed Ethgar," said Arisa. Her voice was cool, but Edoran could hear the effort that kept it so. "Or she ordered it done. Hanging himself in his cell was far too convenient."

Edoran hadn't thought about that. "Because he'd have identified her, to save himself? I don't care much about that, either. He was a traitor to Deorthas, twice over. He'd have been hanged by the courts anyway."

Master Darian had worked for Regent Pettibone, a sin for which Edoran wasn't inclined to forgive anyone. Though he supposed he couldn't hang them all.

"She's not a traitor!" Arisa burst out. "Well, I suppose she is, technically, but she's not evil. She's doing it because she thinks her rule will be better for the people! She believed it was her duty to overthrow Pettibone, and when he was killed . . . Destroying

Pettibone, avenging my father and all the other naval officers he hanged—it had consumed her whole life. Then it happened so fast. . . . I don't think she realized she could quit. But I can convince her to stop now. When I talk to her."

"I have no problem with that," Edoran repeated. In truth, he understood the Falcon. The coup in which Pettibone had seized Deorthas' throne had been much bloodier than the coup that overthrew him. And Pettibone's coup had started with Edoran's father's death, whatever the official investigation had said.

"It's not just vengeance," Arisa persisted. "She really intends to rule well. For the sake of the people."

This wasn't much comfort to Edoran; some of the greatest villains in Deorthas' history had loved their dog, or their horse, or their mother. Pettibone himself had worked with the church to help feed and educate the city poor, and forced factory owners to improve conditions for their workers.

The fact that he'd done a few good deeds hadn't stopped him from killing anyone who stood in his way, including the king. Edoran thought the Falcon was just as ruthless, but he knew better than to say that to her daughter—who, judging by the way she was protesting, seemed to know it anyway in her heart.

"We'd better do something about shelter," he said instead. "It's going to start raining in . . . a bit less than an hour, now."

Arisa shook her head. "It's just weird how you do that. I don't have a tent."

But she'd seen him predict the weather correctly before, so she gathered up her gear without further comment. She also took the time to thoroughly douse the fire, though Edoran, waiting impatiently, didn't see why that was so important.

"Where are we going?" he demanded, when they finally set off. "Is there a farmhouse nearby?"

Arisa snorted. "If there was, would I have been camping out?"

"How should I know?" Edoran asked. "You might have been trying to hide the sword and shield or something."

"I could hide them in the woods before approaching the house," said Arisa. "And then go back for them. That's what I did when I went into town to buy a meal and some camp food."

Edoran frowned. "If you set off a full night ahead of me, how come you're no farther along?"

"Because I had to sleep sometime," Arisa told him. "And because I had to leave the road to check one of our message drops."

"Message drops?" Edoran asked. They were emerging from the trees onto the road. The moonlight coated everything with silver; if he hadn't been so tired and sore, he would have thought the night was beautiful. The storm would come soon. The sky above them was still clear, but clouds obscured the stars in the south. And why hadn't Arisa answered him?

"If we had to move camp, or lost contact with one of our men for any reason, there were a number of places we'd leave messages for them," Arisa told him finally. "I'm pretty sure that's how my mother intended to contact me, when Holis was ready to negotiate."

"Oh." That had been when the Falcon thought she'd have the prince in her hands, instead of Justice Holis' lowborn clerk, though she'd still want to contact her daughter.

Edoran had considered his own childhood a strange one, but Arisa's, growing up in a series of rebel camps, had been even more peculiar. On the other hand, she'd had at least one parent who'd loved and trusted her, and Edoran hadn't.

"So where are we going to find shelter?" he asked. Edoran thought they were now walking west, back toward the city.

"In that shed you told me about," said Arisa. "Where else?"

Edoran stopped walking. It took her a moment to notice and return to him.

"What?" she asked. "You're not afraid of the shed, are you?" *You big baby*, her tone added, but for once Edoran didn't care.

"Suppose they come back?"

"Why should they? They've already taken everything you had. If they wanted to kill you, they'd have done it before they left."

"But there's no hay there or anything. There's nothing there."

"There are four walls and a roof," Arisa pointed out. "According to what you say, we're going to need that, so come on."

She walked off, and Edoran had to jog to catch up with her.

The shed, when they reached it, wasn't quite as frightening as he remembered, but the wood floor was just as uncomfortable, even with Arisa's blankets beneath them.

"Stop turning over," Arisa told him. "You're not going to find a softer spot."

"You were the one who insisted we share the bed," Edoran reminded her.

"There weren't enough blankets for two beds. We'd both have

frozen. Just relax. You've got to be tired. If you'd stop fussing, you'd probably be asleep in minutes."

Edoran sighed. "If you think I can sleep under these conditions, you're out of—"

Thunder interrupted him, and the flare of lightning through the cracks in the walls illuminated the shed's drab interior. It was rough and dirty, and the remains of his possessions were strewn over the floor . . . but there were no lurking bandits. No danger. Rain drummed on the roof.

"It probably leaks," Edoran said. He inched over till his back lay against hers. It wasn't comfortable, but it was warmer. The fury of the storm was impersonal, and somehow soothing.

"We'll know soon," Arisa told him sleepily.

The next time Edoran opened his eyes, it was morning.

The roof had leaked, he noticed. Or perhaps that puddle had come through the cracks in the wall, which now admitted the light of the rising sun. At least it hadn't leaked on him. The blankets wrapped around him still held her body's warmth, but the girl had managed to leave both bed and shed without waking him.

Birds twittered in the fields outside, and Edoran felt a sudden burst of optimism. He'd survived the night—and there'd been times when that hadn't seemed likely! His good spirits lasted right up to the moment he tried to move.

"Ow!" Edoran exclaimed, for perhaps the twentieth time.

"Stop whining," Arisa told him. "Walking will make you feel better, once your muscles warm up."

Edoran pulled the blanket he was using as a shawl a bit tighter, but drafts still leaked up from the bottom. He was beginning to feel better, but he thought he had a right to whine a little bit. If he was back at the palace, he'd have ordered a hot bath, perhaps followed by a massage. Even the meanest peasant would have put some arnica salve on bruises like Edoran's—which in the light of day were quite spectacular. On the other hand, Arisa had replaced the inner soles in his boots, and also rigged him a rough belt from some twine she'd found in the shed, so he probably shouldn't complain for too much longer.

"What are we going to do now?" he asked. "Keep following the troop and see if they lead us to your mother? Or check another of those message drops of yours?"

"Those troops couldn't find my mother for over a decade when they worked for Pettibone," Arisa said. "What makes you think they can find her now? Besides, I think the men she sent out of the city were just a diversion. I think she escaped by sea and probably took Weasel with her. But I know all her old hideouts, and she'll be trying to contact me. I can find her. You're going back to the palace. I'll leave you with the guard in the first town we come to, and they'll see you back. You'll be warm and comfortable in just a few hours, Your Highness. So stop moaning."

"Wait!" Edoran stopped walking. This time she didn't even pause, and he had to scramble to catch up. "I want to go with you! No more whining. I promise."

He'd have sworn the corners of her mouth twitched up, but she suppressed her smile swiftly.

"It's not that," she told him. "I'm accustomed to hearing you whine. There are several reasons I can't take you. Real ones."

"Like what?" Edoran demanded.

"Well, I'll leave aside the fact that Holis must be out of his mind with worry by now. And that if you get killed, there could be a civil war over who gets to be king instead. Because frankly, I don't care about either of those things. You can't come with me because first, all the guardsmen in Deorthas are about to start looking for you. They'd never be able to find my mother, but with you . . . Even if they don't get lucky, they'd get in my way. Second, as soon as it becomes known that you're missing—and don't think that news won't get around—all the villains in Deorthas will start looking for you too. And they're a lot smarter than the guards. I don't want to be rescuing you all the time."

"I can rescue myself," Edoran protested.

"Third," she continued, "you'd slow me down."

Edoran winced. She probably would travel faster without him.

"And fourth," she finished, "if my mother gets hold of you, along with the shield and sword, I'm not sure I could talk her out of trying to seize the throne after all. Because with you in her hands, she'd win!"

That silenced Edoran. She was right. But he wasn't as convinced as she was that her mother could elude the guard. And while the Falcon might listen to Arisa, and would pay no attention to anything Edoran said, if the Falcon ever got herself trapped, the guards and shareholders who were dealing with her would simply ignore Arisa . . . and they might be forced to listen to their prince. It was going to take both of them, but Edoran had heard her use that decided tone before—she wasn't interested in any arguments he might make.

Did she want to be the one to rescue Weasel herself? She'd been jealous of Weasel's friendship with the prince. To be honest, he'd been jealous of Weasel's friendship with her. So did *he* want to be the one to save Weasel? He did, but if it came down to it, he'd put Weasel's safety first.

Was she right? Would it be better for Weasel if he went back?

No. He was oddly sure of that. Arisa saw her mother through eyes blinded by pride and love. But he'd never be able to persuade her of that, either.

So how to convince her to take him along? He couldn't run off and find the Falcon himself. Even if she hadn't escaped by sea, Edoran was clearly hopeless on his own. But the only thing he'd ever seen this stubborn girl pay attention to, besides her mother, was . . .

The familiar sinking in his stomach chilled him. But it was something she might heed. And seeing his future laid out wouldn't kill him. It wasn't as if he hadn't seen it a dozen times before.

"Do you have your arcanara deck in that pack?" Edoran asked.

"Sure," Arisa told him. "I figured I'd need all the guidance I could get. Why?"

"Seek guidance now," said Edoran. "Ask the cards if you should take me with you."

"I already know the answer to that. I don't bother the cards about something I already know."

"I'll bet you don't know," Edoran told her. "In fact, I'll make you a wager. You let me shuffle that deck. If the tower turns up as the threat, you'll take me with you."

Arisa laughed. "If sending you back made the tower come up as the threat, I'd take you with me, bet or no bet. The tower's the worst card in the deck. It's not just death, it's the destruction of all you hold dear. The tower signifies the destruction of your whole world."

Her voice was even, but the freckles stood out on her pale cheeks. Edoran wondered if she'd cast the cards on the night she'd learned of her mother's plot. Her own world had certainly shattered.

"So take the wager," he said. "If the tower does turn up, you won't have to do anything you wouldn't do anyway. And if it doesn't, I'll go to the town guard without arguing about it."

He never said he'd *stay* with them, but he doubted it would come to that. He'd seen the arcanara cards at work too often.

Arisa eyed him oddly. "You hate the cards. You don't believe in them."

"But you do," said Edoran. "Try."

Arisa had finally stopped walking. "If the tower doesn't come up as the threat, you'll go to the guard without any argument?"

"That's right."

"Then that's got to be worth it. But I warn you, the odds are fifty-three to one in my favor."

Edoran only smiled.

It took some time to find a rock flat enough to hold the layout, but the morning sun had already dried it. Edoran folded his blanket to sit on while Arisa pulled the deck from the depths of her pack and shuffled it once. Then she passed it to Edoran. "Your turn."

He shuffled three times, though that was probably unnecessary. He only had to touch the cards, sometimes just be in the same room, to affect them.

So it didn't worry him when she took the deck and shuffled once more herself. In fact, he almost laughed. Did she really think he was such a skilled cardsharp that he could stack the deck as he shuffled it?

"My question is: Should I send this worthless prince back to his palace?" Arisa intoned.

Edoran grimaced, but it wouldn't matter how she phrased it, or even what she asked.

"This is my significator," she went on. "The card that represents me."

She set the first card in the center of the rock, and stared at the fool's bright motley in astonishment. "But my card is the storm!"

Edoran's breath trickled out in a sigh, and she frowned at him.

"This supports me," she said. "This I can rely on."

"Chaos." Edoran spoke before she even lifted the card from the deck, long before she turned it over. Her eyes widened with astonishment.

"How did you do that?"

He shrugged. "I won't do it again."

In truth, he couldn't, for the other cards changed. All except chaos and the tower. Because the fool wasn't her card. It was his.

"This inspires me," said Arisa slowly. She laid down a picture of an old man and a babe, spinning the world between them. "Time. The past creating the present. If you've got nothing to rely on except chaos, time probably would inspire you. But that's not me!" She stared at the fool once more.

"Get to it," Edoran told her. "You're about to lose."

Arisa scowled. "This threatens me." She turned the next card.

Edoran looked at the gray stone tower, collapsing into rubble as flames shot from its roof, and tried not to smirk.

"How are you doing this?" Arisa demanded.

"So you'll take me?"

"I guess I have to." Her gaze went to the tower, and her lips tightened. "It looks like I'd better. This will protect me."

She laid the wedding between the tower and the fool.

"Alliances of all kinds." She looked at Edoran over the cards, then shrugged. "This misleads me." She placed the brimming cornucopia to the fool's far right.

Edoran didn't comment on that. It had always been clear to him that returning to the comforts of the palace would be a mistake.

"And this guides me true." She set the farmer, tending his crop, between abundance and the fool. "It looks like one of us has some growing to do." Her glance was very sharp.

"We'll probably have the chance for it," Edoran agreed blandly. "Traveling together and all."

Arisa sighed. "You won. You don't have to rub it in."

They'd walked for almost an hour, mostly in silence, before she asked him, "How did you know that the tower would turn up?"

Edoran smiled grimly. "I don't believe in the cards."

CHAPTER 4

JUSTICE

Justice: the balancing of the scales.
May indicate either punishment
or a voluntary act of contrition.

They came to a town at midmorning, and Arisa assigned Edoran to carry the sword and shield along the paths and back roads around it and meet her on the other side.

Edoran protested that every carter who'd passed them this morning had already seen them. Arisa replied that in just a few hours, days at most, those carters would be somewhere else, almost impossible for a troop of guardsmen to question, while the townsfolk would be right there—perfectly willing to tell the troop's captain about the young girl who'd come through lugging an antique shield and sword . . . and the boy who'd traveled with her.

Edoran then proposed that they wrap the sword and shield in blankets, or disguise them some other way. Arisa invited him to try, and spent the next ten minutes chuckling at his attempt to conceal two distinctively shaped objects, one almost four feet long and the other a bit longer.

He managed to wrap the blankets around them, but the result was a bundle so awkward that it would attract as much attention as carrying the shield and sword openly.

"Look at it this way," Arisa told him, as he struggled to return the blankets to their neat roll. "If you weren't here, I'd have to carry them around myself, then go back into town to find out about the troop, and then drag them out of hiding before I went on—so instead of slowing us down, you're saving me time."

It wasn't much consolation to Edoran, as he carried them along the paths that ran between the fields. Arisa had rigged straps to hang both sword and shield over his shoulders, and the sword wasn't too uncomfortable. But even with the blanket to cushion his back, the shield was hard-edged, heavy, and awkward. Edoran was sweating by the time he found the place she'd described, where a stone wall surrounded a small orchard.

As he thankfully shed his burden and settled in to wait, it occurred to Edoran that she'd been carrying these things not only all morning, but all day yesterday as well. She really was an amazing girl.

He began to think her somewhat less amazing as the minutes dragged past, but he forgave her when she turned up carrying not only a fresh loaf of bread, but a hot sausage whose scent filled the air before she even unwrapped it.

"I bought you a coat as well." She indicated a lump of rough brown wool and patches. More patches than wool, as far as Edoran could see.

"That's a coat?"

"It's warmer than what you've got now. And it was cheap," Arisa told him. "I *think* it's even clean. You can't wander around wrapped in a blanket; people will notice. And that's important," she added. "Because they're looking for you."

Edoran abandoned his half of the sausage, suddenly less hungry. "Already?"

"The guards passed me as I was going into the town. Palace guards." Arisa's voice was properly grim, but her eyes were bright with the thrill of the hunt. "I'd pulled my hair back and tucked it into my collar, so there was almost no chance they'd recognize me." She still wore her dark red hair that way, and unless they looked closely anyone would take her for a boy—particularly men who'd previously seen her wearing the gowns of a fine lady. "I managed to get close enough to overhear when they stopped in the main square to question people," she went on. "It was you they were looking for. It's a good thing you're such an unremarkable little shrimp. Brown hair and brown eyes are no good at all as a description."

Edoran clutched his blanket tighter. "We got lucky. If they'd come up with us on the road . . ."

"Then we'd have hidden in a ditch or a hedge," Arisa told him. "I've been listening for a troop behind us all morning, and they're riding fast enough that I promise we'd hear them before they saw us. But I don't think you have as much to worry about as you think you do."

"Why?" Worrying seemed perfectly sensible to him.

"Because they're looking for 'a young noble, fifteen years old, in a good brown worsted suit and a gray cloak lined with rabbit fur.' Your valet knew what you were wearing, didn't he?"

"He saw me packing." A wave of burning fury washed over Edoran. "But he won't be my valet for one minute after I get home!"

"You can't really blame him," Arisa pointed out. "Justice Holis pays his salary. And what he told them will make you safer, because you look more like a thirteen-year-old ragpicker than a fifteen-year-old nobleman."

Edoran looked down at his collarless shirt and rope-belted britches. Both were more than a little grubby, and the rough coat she'd brought him would complete the image. He regarded it with more favor and took another bite of sausage.

Since Arisa considered Edoran adequately disguised, they kept on the road for the rest of the day and into the evening. It was dark when they finally reached the village where Arisa had decided to stop.

Edoran was grateful for his ragged coat by then, for it was warm, softer than he'd expected, and he was long past caring how he looked. Arisa had carried the sword and shield on the road, but he'd been forced to lug them around so many small villages that he'd have sworn he carried them almost half the time. At least a third. He was more tired than he'd ever been in his life.

He listened with approval as Arisa bargained with the inn-keeper to let them eat their stew before they started working. After all, they couldn't mop the floor or wipe off the tables till the last customers left—though that would probably be soon. There was only one occupied table now; their plates were empty and their mugs were low.

The stew was hot and filling, and Edoran thought it an excellent bargain . . . until Arisa handed him a wet, grubby cloth and told him to clean the tables. "You can get them started while I draw mop water from the well."

She departed before he could force words past his astonishment, and after a moment he was glad. He'd realized that they'd have to work for food and lodging, and he'd promised not to slow her down. Paying for his own dinner and a pallet to spread near the taproom hearth was doubtless part of that bargain. Edoran approached the first table with some trepidation, but he soon discovered that when he swiped the cloth back and forth all of the crumbs fell off the sides and the surface was evenly coated with wetness. And probably clean. Or at least cleaner, for his rag became grubbier as the task went on.

Arisa returned and started mopping the floor. Edoran watched her, surreptitiously, and that didn't look too hard either. It was just a variant of what he was doing, except that her method for spreading wetness was a pack of strings tied to the end of a pole, and she dunked it into the bucket every few minutes and then twisted some of the water out of it against the bucket's edge.

Should he be dunking his rag in something? Surely as the water in the bucket got dirtier and dirtier, she was just spreading—

"What are you doing?" Arisa snapped. "I just cleaned that!"

"What?" Edoran looked around. He was standing on an area she'd mopped, but he had to stand there to reach the table.

"You dropped that pile of crumbs onto the floor I just cleaned," said Arisa angrily. "Which means I'll have to do it again. You haven't been knocking all the crumbs onto the floor, have you?"

Her eyes had narrowed in suspicion, but Edoran didn't know what she was accusing him of.

"When you clean them off the table, the crumbs fall on the floor," he pointed out. "Where do you expect them to go? To the ceiling?"

Arisa closed her eyes, took a deep breath, and opened them again. "You're supposed to catch them in your hand before they hit the floor," she told him. "Like this."

She took the cloth and wiped a pile of crumbs, pipe ash, and the One God alone knew what into her waiting palm. Then she went and emptied her hand into the hearth and came back. She handed Edoran the cloth.

He stared at her in disgust. "You expect me to take such stuff into my bare hand? Under no circumstances!" Touching the rag was bad enough, but he'd tried not to think about that.

Arisa sighed. "Maybe we should switch jobs. With a mop, you won't have to touch anything but the handle."

She sounded patient and obliging, but there was a glint in her eyes that Edoran didn't trust. Still, he'd watched her for some time, and it hadn't appeared difficult.

He soon realized why she'd offered to swap, for working the stick was harder than wiping the tables. And a large part of that effort consisted of dunking the mop and twisting it against the side of the bucket, which made no sense to Edoran. The water went back onto the floor anyway. It would surely save a great deal of time to dump it straight onto the floor, sop it up with the mop, and then twist it into the bucket. And he was tired. If there was a shortcut, Edoran was prepared to take it.

He poured out almost three-fourths of the bucket in an arc across the floor. When Arisa shrieked he jumped, and the last of it splashed out.

"Now what?" he asked impatiently.

He soon found out what, for returning large amounts of water to the bucket turned out to be trickier than he'd expected. Even when they finished mopping, and then wiped the floor with cloths from the kitchen, the rough wood was still so damp that Arisa insisted on keeping the window open so it would be dry by morning.

This made for a chilly night, despite the hearth fire. Edoran was yawning and bleary-eyed when they set off again, shortly after sunrise.

Arisa, also yawning, said nothing more about the incident. But her silence was almost as eloquent as her previous curses.

If they looked even half as tired and bedraggled as Edoran felt, it was no wonder that the carter who'd slowly pulled past them stopped his ox team and called back, "I'm headed into Mallerton. You two want a ride?"

Every aching muscle in Edoran's body screamed, *Yes!* But Arisa hesitated.

"We'd not want t' burden your beasts," she said, her strong country accent warning Edoran to keep his mouth shut.

"No problem for them, lass. My cargo today is fine glass panes packed in straw. The glass is heavy enough, but the straw around it weighs practically nothing—and it's the greater part of the load. Joss and Shem here could carry ten of the two of you and hardly feel it."

She hesitated still, and Edoran gave her a nudge in the ribs with his elbow. *Say yes!*

Arisa glared at him, then turned back to the carter. "We'll accept your offer, goodman, with thanks t' you and your beasts."

They scrambled onto the cart and found themselves places in the space between the crates. Then the oxen set off at their slow walk—far slower than a horse, Edoran noted. The fact that they'd passed Edoran and Arisa on the road told Edoran how slowly they'd been walking, and he sighed and leaned against the side of the wagon.

"I thank you, too, goodman." He tried to mimic Arisa's accent, but he must not have succeeded, for the driver glanced at him in mild surprise.

"He's just back from a stay in the city," Arisa told him. "A long stay, for his mam sent him to learn accounting, but he wasn't any good at it."

"I was too," Edoran retorted, stung. Why did she always have to make him out a fool? He wasn't good with numbers, but until Holis' new tutors had arrived, no one had ever tried to teach him.

The carter looked at Edoran's clothes and face, and a frown creased his broad forehead. "You been robbed, lad? Whitston's the next town, and I can take you straight to the town guard's office. It's only a bit off the main street, no trouble at all."

"No!" said Edoran sharply. "I mean, I wasn't robbed. I, ah . . ."

"He means that when his master turned him off he was fool enough to take up gambling," said Arisa, with all the righteousness of a good sibling ratting out an erring brother. "And with the wrong people, too. They did that to him when he couldn't pay his debts, so then he finally wrote home and Aunt Allie—he's my cousin, you see—she sent me to bring him back. But I'm the

one with the purse, and you can bet I'm keeping a close eye on it."
She shot him a look so smug that Edoran didn't know whether he
wanted to smack her or burst into applause.

"Why, you . . . That's . . . You don't have to tell people that!" he
burst out indignantly.

The carter laughed. "Don't let it trouble you too much, lad.
Youth's the time to make mistakes, while you can still recover
from them. But I asked about robbers," he went on, "because those
accursed pirates have been raiding farther and farther inland.
Though if you'd fallen foul of them, you'd likely be dead," he finished grimly. "Not just a bit bruised."

Edoran wondered if the carter had heard the rumors he'd
started at the gates, but Arisa said soberly, "I heard they hit Tisdale,
but I'd hoped that was wrong. It's almost twenty miles from the
coast!"

"It's small and rich," said the carter. "What with all those
potteries. And because it's so far inland the guards weren't even
trying to cover it. Last count I heard was eighteen dead, but
those numbers sometimes grow in the telling. We can hope it's
fewer."

He seemed certain that some had died. And Arisa had already
heard of the Tisdale raid? When? Why hadn't she told him?

Edoran glared at her but she ignored him, talking to the carter
instead. Perhaps she thought his erratic gift might have given him
some warning, but it hadn't, not since that first raid—and given
how that had felt, Edoran could only be grateful.

The sun was warm despite the chill air, and the jouncing of the cart didn't prevent Edoran's eyelids from drooping. It wouldn't hurt to rest his eyes for a while. . . .

A particularly bad jolt woke him. A glance at the sun told him that only a few hours had passed, but the hard edges of the wagon and crate were biting into his flesh, and an urgent bodily need was making itself felt.

"Pull over, goodman," he said. "I need to . . . I must attend to business."

The man shot him a startled glance, but then he laughed. "I could stand to attend to that business myself."

They were coming up on a wider place in the road, and he guided the oxen into it and stopped. Edoran clambered over the side and found some bushes to give him privacy. The man still hadn't returned when he climbed back into the cart and turned to meet Arisa's scowl.

"Talk to him like a man!" she hissed. "He's not your servant!"

Edoran frowned. He'd spoken perfectly politely. He'd even remembered to address the man as goodman, in the country manner. He was about to ask what she was talking about when the carter came back, and they couldn't discuss that in his presence.

So Edoran shut his mouth and passed the rest of the journey to Mallerton glaring at Arisa. They reached the town a bit before dusk, and the carter dropped them off. Edoran echoed Arisa's thanks—graciously!—then turned to her and whispered, "What were you talking about? I was perfectly polite!"

Arisa rolled her eyes. "For someone addressing his inferior.

Never mind. I know you don't understand. You probably can't, and we're both too tired to discuss it. We'd end up quarreling, and there's no point. It'll be dark in an hour, and I need light to find the next message drop. I'm going to see if there's some inn that will give us real beds in exchange for a hand with the dinner dishes. Even you couldn't screw up drying a dish!"

She turned and walked off before he could reply, which was probably just as well. That short speech had held so many insults, Edoran wasn't sure which he should respond to first.

The third inn they tried was shorthanded in the kitchen, and several of their smaller rooms were empty, so Arisa struck the bargain she wanted. Soon Edoran was standing in front of a tub of very hot water with a drying cloth in his hand. At least this time the cloth was clean.

"I'll wash," said Arisa, gesturing to the tub in front of her, which had soap bubbles on its murky surface. "When I hand you a dish, you dip it into the rinse water, dry it off with the cloth, then stack it on the board beside the tub. Clear?"

"Perfectly," said Edoran crossly. The very care with which she explained was an insult, but for all the clamor of cooks, waitresses, and tapsters rushing about, he didn't dare argue with her publicly.

In truth, the bustling kitchen was a bit intimidating, but dipping the plates and drying them was so simple that he soon got ahead of her, and found himself waiting for the next one.

Arisa observed his smug glance. "Washing is always slower than drying," she told him.

"If you say so," said Edoran, "I'm sure it's true. Particularly when you're the one doing the wash—"

"What's this?" One of the cooks, a big-boned woman with strands of hair curling wildly around the edge of her cap, was frowning at him. She was holding out a plate, pointing to the edge, where a triangle of soap scum made a swirling pattern on the porcelain glaze.

"That's where I held the plate to dip it into the water," Edoran told her. Politely. "It was too hot to put my hand in."

The woman's face turned red. She seemed to be trying to speak.

"I'm sorry, mistress," said Arisa hastily. Edoran noted that she used the city term, which implied that the woman she spoke to outranked her. "He's simple sometimes about things like that. We'll do them over, and I'll keep an eye on him to be certain they're done right."

The woman studied Edoran, no doubt looking for some outward sign of his feeble wits. "See that you do."

She stalked off, and Edoran glared at Arisa. "Now what?"

"You have to rinse the *whole* plate, you . . . you half-wit!" she snarled.

"But the water's too hot. It would scald me."

"It's supposed to be hot! You take the plate and turn it in the water, like this."

She dipped the rim of the plate into the tub, turning it till the whole surface had been submerged.

"When we do the glasses and mugs you do the same, rinsing

them inside and out before you dry them. And when we do flat-ware, you drop the whole thing into the water, then use something with a long handle to fish it back out."

"Oh. Why didn't you explain that before?"

"Because I hadn't realized how hopeless you really are. Do these again." She pointed to the stack of plates he'd just finished. "I'll do some pots next. They take a bit of scrubbing, so it'll give you time to catch up."

By the time the kitchen closed for the night, Edoran was too weary to argue about insults or anything else. In his opinion, working was vastly overrated. Particularly as a way to build char-acter, for everyone who engaged in it was far too snappish and fussy, and seemed to have no manners at all. He was particularly tired of Arisa snapping at him, and insulting him, and leading him around by the hand as if he was a toddler! He'd have rescued himself if she hadn't been there, for the night hadn't been cold enough to freeze to death after all.

The narrow feather tick in the small attic room was a blessing for his aching bones, and he hardly had the strength to pull off his boots, much less go to her room and start a fight, before sleep claimed him.

He woke at dawn the next morning and lay still for a time, enjoying the solitude as much as the warm bed.

He probably shouldn't argue with Arisa. He was hopeless at this working thing, which had turned out to be much more complex than it looked. She was keeping her promise to take him along, even though he knew he was slowing her. And every guard in the realm was now on his trail, just as she'd prophesied. He'd have to take great care to keep himself out of the Falcon's hands when they found her—it would be disastrous if that prophecy came true.

He donned his now really dirty clothes and went to tap on Arisa's door.

She seemed subdued that day as well, and they made good time to the message drop—which, to Edoran's disappointment, proved to be nothing more than a rotted hollow, high in a tree by the crossing of a couple of back roads. It was empty.

Arisa was frowning as she climbed down. "It may be too soon. She knows where I'll be checking, and there are four other drops along this route. She may not be settled into hiding yet. Or even have decided what she wants to do next, since she's only got Weasel instead of you."

"I suppose that did put a crimp in her plan." Edoran tried to keep his voice neutral, but Arisa cast him a sharp look anyway. It faded into a sigh.

She was the one who had thwarted her mother's plan.

"Come on," she told him. "The next drop is two days' walk from here."

Edoran didn't know if they passed the town they should have stopped at, or failed to reach some place Arisa had intended to stay, but when the sun started down they were nowhere near a town, or even a village.

"Curse it," Arisa muttered, staring at the wilderness around them. Even the plowed fields were scarce here, and the woods around the road made the evening shadows deeper. "If it was summer, we'd still have two or three hours of daylight!"

"Well, it's not, and we don't," Edoran told her, trying not to snap. "What do we do now?"

"Make camp here." She gestured to a clearing, a bit off the road. Judging by the old fire rings, it had been used for that purpose before, but it looked remarkably bare of comforts to Edoran. On the other hand, he didn't have a better idea.

At Arisa's insistence, he went out to gather wood for the fire. It had been mostly dry weather for the past week, but the persistent rain before that had soaked everything thoroughly, and it was harder to find dry wood than he'd expected. He brought back a respectable armload and was irritated when she sent him out for another. And another. By the time he'd gathered enough to keep the fire going all night, the pile was almost as high as his head, and it was too dark to search further.

But in the time he'd been looking she'd built a crackling fire, fetched water from the stream, laid out a thick pallet of cut pine boughs, and made hot tea in her tin water flask. Edoran thought that was quite ingenious, though she had to wrap her coat sleeve around her hand to pick it up and pour.

"Why did you pack two mugs?" he asked, accepting his gratefully.

"I didn't. I bought it when I bought your coat," she told him. "Along with another bowl and spoon, though we've nothing to go in the bowls but bread and cheese again."

The mug she was using had a broken handle, and Edoran deduced that it was the one she'd purchased—she'd given the good one to him. "Bread and cheese will be fine. How much farther to this next drop of yours? Will we make it—"

"Your Highness!"

A loud rustling in the brush accompanied the half shout, and Edoran jumped, spilling his tea. A knife appeared in Arisa's hand.

"Thank the One God I've found you!"

The man who led his horse out of the bushes was only medium height, but he was as lean as one of his own blades and moved like an acrobat. The horse was sweat-stained and weary. But it didn't surprise Edoran that Master Giles would override a horse.

"How did you find us?" he stammered. Cold dismay ran through his nerves, paralyzing his wits.

"With great difficulty, Your Highness," Edoran's fencing master replied. "It was sheer luck that I encountered a farmer who'd seen you in the company of a red-haired boy—or at least, two boys traveling together, one with red hair. But I remembered Mistress Benison's penchant for britches, and since I knew she was missing, I thought you might be together. They remembered her in the town markets," he went on smugly. "Though you did a remarkable job of eluding their attention. But that doesn't matter now—you'll soon be back in the palace, safe and sound."

Arisa was watching him with narrowed eyes. "All that searching must have taken you at least a few days, even on horseback, and we've only been gone for four. How did you find out that the prince was missing so quickly?"

Edoran blinked. In his astonishment he'd forgotten that Giles was his *ex*-fencing-master. He'd been fired by Justice Holis, along with the rest of Edoran's tutors, when Holis learned that Pettibone had paid them not to teach the prince, but to make it as difficult as they could for him to learn anything. And Giles had enjoyed humiliating him even more than the others.

Edoran tried to steady his quaking will. His stomach churned and ached in a way it hadn't since he'd left the palace—not even when he'd been in terror for his life from the robbers. That was odd, but he had no time to think about it now.

"I'm not going back," Edoran told the man who'd intimidated him from the day he was old enough to hold a blade. "You're no longer my tutor. You have no authority over me. Not anymore."

Master Giles' expression of happy greeting faded into the familiar arrogance.

"It might be argued that the reward Holis has offered for your safe return gives any man in the kingdom the right to bring you back. But authority isn't really the issue, is it?"

He meant that he could outfight Edoran with one hand behind his back and one eye closed—he'd proved it over and over on the salle floor. There was a rapier in a scabbard on his belt, the hilts of two more protruded from the pack on his horse's rump, and he was one of the best swordsmen in all Deorthas. He could compel Edoran to do anything he wanted.

But Arisa had risen to her feet—and she still held the knife. Which was ridiculous, for even Arisa was no match for Giles in a straight-up fight. He'd proved that, too.

"I don't believe Holis issued a reward," she said. "He wouldn't dare admit the prince was missing."

"He didn't have much choice." Giles pulled a length of cord from his saddlebag, just right for binding someone's wrists. The sight filled Edoran with dread.

"You don't have to use that," he protested. "I know I can't fight you."

Which didn't mean he couldn't run . . . unless Giles actually tied him up. Would he dare? Why not? Edoran would never forgive him anyway, so he had nothing to lose.

"What do you mean, Holis had no choice?" Arisa asked.

"Rumors that the prince has vanished have spread throughout the court," Giles told them. "Since Holis couldn't produce the prince to refute them, he gave up, admitted it, and offered a reward for his return. He's still trying to keep the news from the populace, though I doubt that will be possible much longer. But no one's offering any money for you, girl, so if you trouble me . . ."

It was only then that his gaze fell on the sword and shield. His mouth opened and closed several times before he found his voice. "You stole them?"

If he hadn't felt so wretched, Edoran would have grinned.

Then Giles' eyes narrowed. "You really were working with your mother. I commend you, girl. I didn't believe it."

"She was not!" Edoran exclaimed.

"Believe what you like," Arisa snapped. "You have no authority over me or Edoran, and you're not taking either of us anywhere."

"But I am," said Giles. "His Highness, and the sword and shield,

are all going right back to the palace, where they belong."

Edoran couldn't have said what subtle shift in the man's expression gave him away, but suddenly he knew. "He's lying! He has no intention of taking me back."

Giles smiled. "Well, it occurs to me that there might be people who'd pay more for you than Holis would, especially with the sword and shield as part of the package. The three of you together . . . I'd be offering the whole throne of Deorthas, for sale to the highest bidder."

Arisa leaped at him, but he'd clearly been expecting it—his rapier sprang from the scabbard, swiping her blade aside. That wouldn't have mattered so much, but the hard kick to the wrist that followed it broke her grip and sent the knife spinning into the darkness.

"Bad move, girl." Giles' smile now was the one Edoran used to see when he'd angered his tutor in some small way. That smile meant a beating that would leave him sore for days, but that left no bruise he could complain about. "I have no quarrel with you," the fencing master continued, "but I have no need to keep you alive, either."

"You do if you want to sell Edoran to my mother. You need me to act as a go-between." Arisa was clutching her wrist, but her back was straight. Her plain face, in the flickering light, seemed cast in steel. "You won't even be able to contact her without me."

If she could fight on, with no weapon but her wits . . .

The idea that came to Edoran then made his blood run cold—but what choice did he have? Giles would never let him escape,

but he couldn't kill him either. The sword and shield were far less important than capturing the prince. And Arisa was of no importance at all.

If he thought about it, he might lose his nerve. And it was time Edoran rescued something!

Two swift steps took him to the horse. The sound of a rapier rasping free of its sheath made Giles turn. His eyes flickered, but he didn't look too surprised. And not at all frightened, curse him.

Though Edoran had to admit, Giles didn't have much to be frightened of.

"Take the sword and shield and run," Edoran told Arisa. "I can delay him for a few moments, at least."

Master Giles laughed.

Arisa didn't.

"What about you? I promised—"

"I release you from it," said Edoran. "Get the sword and shield away—"

Giles suddenly saw that he meant it. He turned his back on Edoran and took a step toward the gear pile, where the sword and shield lay.

Edoran ran forward, ready—absolutely ready, he promised himself—to run the sword in his hand right through Giles' back and out the other side. He was so frightened and furious that he might even have done it. He would never know, because as the sharp point neared him the fencing master spun, knocking Edoran's blade wide.

The blow was so hard, it almost jarred the hilt from his hand.

are all going right back to the palace, where they belong."

Edoran couldn't have said what subtle shift in the man's expression gave him away, but suddenly he knew. "He's lying! He has no intention of taking me back."

Giles smiled. "Well, it occurs to me that there might be people who'd pay more for you than Holis would, especially with the sword and shield as part of the package. The three of you together . . . I'd be offering the whole throne of Deorthas, for sale to the highest bidder."

Arisa leaped at him, but he'd clearly been expecting it—his rapier sprang from the scabbard, swiping her blade aside. That wouldn't have mattered so much, but the hard kick to the wrist that followed it broke her grip and sent the knife spinning into the darkness.

"Bad move, girl." Giles' smile now was the one Edoran used to see when he'd angered his tutor in some small way. That smile meant a beating that would leave him sore for days, but that left no bruise he could complain about. "I have no quarrel with you," the fencing master continued, "but I have no need to keep you alive, either."

"You do if you want to sell Edoran to my mother. You need me to act as a go-between." Arisa was clutching her wrist, but her back was straight. Her plain face, in the flickering light, seemed cast in steel. "You won't even be able to contact her without me."

If she could fight on, with no weapon but her wits . . .

The idea that came to Edoran then made his blood run cold— but what choice did he have? Giles would never let him escape,

but he couldn't kill him either. The sword and shield were far less important than capturing the prince. And Arisa was of no importance at all.

If he thought about it, he might lose his nerve. And it was time Edoran rescued something!

Two swift steps took him to the horse. The sound of a rapier rasping free of its sheath made Giles turn. His eyes flickered, but he didn't look too surprised. And not at all frightened, curse him.

Though Edoran had to admit, Giles didn't have much to be frightened of.

"Take the sword and shield and run," Edoran told Arisa. "I can delay him for a few moments, at least."

Master Giles laughed.

Arisa didn't.

"What about you? I promised—"

"I release you from it," said Edoran. "Get the sword and shield away—"

Giles suddenly saw that he meant it. He turned his back on Edoran and took a step toward the gear pile, where the sword and shield lay.

Edoran ran forward, ready—absolutely ready, he promised himself—to run the sword in his hand right through Giles and out the other side. He was so frightened and furious that he might even have done it. He would never know, because as the sharp point neared him the fencing master spun, knocking Edoran's blade wide.

The blow was so hard, it almost jarred the hilt from his

are all going right back to the palace, where they belong."

Edoran couldn't have said what subtle shift in the man's expression gave him away, but suddenly he knew. "He's lying! He has no intention of taking me back."

Giles smiled. "Well, it occurs to me that there might be people who'd pay more for you than Holis would, especially with the sword and shield as part of the package. The three of you together . . . I'd be offering the whole throne of Deorthas, for sale to the highest bidder."

Arisa leaped at him, but he'd clearly been expecting it—his rapier sprang from the scabbard, swiping her blade aside. That wouldn't have mattered so much, but the hard kick to the wrist that followed it broke her grip and sent the knife spinning into the darkness.

"Bad move, girl." Giles' smile now was the one Edoran used to see when he'd angered his tutor in some small way. That smile meant a beating that would leave him sore for days, but that left no bruise he could complain about. "I have no quarrel with you," the fencing master continued, "but I have no need to keep you alive, either."

"You do if you want to sell Edoran to my mother. You need me to act as a go-between." Arisa was clutching her wrist, but her back was straight. Her plain face, in the flickering light, seemed cast in steel. "You won't even be able to contact her without me."

If she could fight on, with no weapon but her wits . . .

The idea that came to Edoran then made his blood run cold—but what choice did he have? Giles would never let him escape,

but he couldn't kill him either. The sword and shield were far less important than capturing the prince. And Arisa was of no importance at all.

If he thought about it, he might lose his nerve. And it was time Edoran rescued something!

Two swift steps took him to the horse. The sound of a rapier rasping free of its sheath made Giles turn. His eyes flickered, but he didn't look too surprised. And not at all frightened, curse him.

Though Edoran had to admit, Giles didn't have much to be frightened of.

"Take the sword and shield and run," Edoran told Arisa. "I can delay him for a few moments, at least."

Master Giles laughed.

Arisa didn't.

"What about you? I promised—"

"I release you from it," said Edoran. "Get the sword and shield away—"

Giles suddenly saw that he meant it. He turned his back on Edoran and took a step toward the gear pile, where the sword and shield lay.

Edoran ran forward, ready—absolutely ready, he promised himself—to run the sword in his hand right through Giles' back and out the other side. He was so frightened and furious that he might even have done it. He would never know, because as the sharp point neared him the fencing master spun, knocking Edoran's blade wide.

The blow was so hard, it almost jarred the hilt from his hand.

Edoran blinked. In his astonishment he'd forgotten that Giles was his *ex*-fencing-master. He'd been fired by Justice Holis, along with the rest of Edoran's tutors, when Holis learned that Pettibone had paid them not to teach the prince, but to make it as difficult as they could for him to learn anything. And Giles had enjoyed humiliating him even more than the others.

Edoran tried to steady his quaking will. His stomach churned and ached in a way it hadn't since he'd left the palace—not even when he'd been in terror for his life from the robbers. That was odd, but he had no time to think about it now.

"I'm not going back," Edoran told the man who'd intimidated him from the day he was old enough to hold a blade. "You're no longer my tutor. You have no authority over me. Not anymore."

Master Giles' expression of happy greeting faded into the familiar arrogance.

"It might be argued that the reward Holis has offered for your safe return gives any man in the kingdom the right to bring you back. But authority isn't really the issue, is it?"

He meant that he could outfight Edoran with one hand behind his back and one eye closed—he'd proved it over and over on the salle floor. There was a rapier in a scabbard on his belt, the hilts of two more protruded from the pack on his horse's rump, and he was one of the best swordsmen in all Deorthas. He could compel Edoran to do anything he wanted.

But Arisa had risen to her feet—and she still held the knife. Which was ridiculous, for even Arisa was no match for Giles in a straight-up fight. He'd proved that, too.

"I don't believe Holis issued a reward," she said. "He would n dare admit the prince was missing."

"He didn't have much choice." Giles pulled a length of co from his saddlebag, just right for binding someone's wrists. T sight filled Edoran with dread.

"You don't have to use that," he protested. "I know I can't fi you."

Which didn't mean he couldn't run . . . unless Giles actu tied him up. Would he dare? Why not? Edoran would never give him anyway, so he had nothing to lose.

"What do you mean, Holis had no choice?" Arisa asked.

"Rumors that the prince has vanished have spread throug the court," Giles told them. "Since Holis couldn't produc prince to refute them, he gave up, admitted it, and offered a r for his return. He's still trying to keep the news from the pop though I doubt that will be possible much longer. But no offering any money for you, girl, so if you trouble me . . ."

It was only then that his gaze fell on the sword and shie mouth opened and closed several times before he found hi "You stole them?"

If he hadn't felt so wretched, Edoran would have grin

Then Giles' eyes narrowed. "You really were workin v mother. I commend you, girl. I didn't believe it."

"She was not!" Edoran exclaimed.

"Believe what you like," Arisa snapped. "You have no over me or Edoran, and you're not taking either of us a

"But I am," said Giles. "His Highness, and the sword a

Edoran blinked. In his astonishment he'd forgotten that Giles was his *ex*-fencing-master. He'd been fired by Justice Holis, along with the rest of Edoran's tutors, when Holis learned that Pettibone had paid them not to teach the prince, but to make it as difficult as they could for him to learn anything. And Giles had enjoyed humiliating him even more than the others.

Edoran tried to steady his quaking will. His stomach churned and ached in a way it hadn't since he'd left the palace—not even when he'd been in terror for his life from the robbers. That was odd, but he had no time to think about it now.

"I'm not going back," Edoran told the man who'd intimidated him from the day he was old enough to hold a blade. "You're no longer my tutor. You have no authority over me. Not anymore."

Master Giles' expression of happy greeting faded into the familiar arrogance.

"It might be argued that the reward Holis has offered for your safe return gives any man in the kingdom the right to bring you back. But authority isn't really the issue, is it?"

He meant that he could outfight Edoran with one hand behind his back and one eye closed—he'd proved it over and over on the salle floor. There was a rapier in a scabbard on his belt, the hilts of two more protruded from the pack on his horse's rump, and he was one of the best swordsmen in all Deorthas. He could compel Edoran to do anything he wanted.

But Arisa had risen to her feet—and she still held the knife. Which was ridiculous, for even Arisa was no match for Giles in a straight-up fight. He'd proved that, too.

"I don't believe Holis issued a reward," she said. "He wouldn't dare admit the prince was missing."

"He didn't have much choice." Giles pulled a length of cord from his saddlebag, just right for binding someone's wrists. The sight filled Edoran with dread.

"You don't have to use that," he protested. "I know I can't fight you."

Which didn't mean he couldn't run . . . unless Giles actually tied him up. Would he dare? Why not? Edoran would never forgive him anyway, so he had nothing to lose.

"What do you mean, Holis had no choice?" Arisa asked.

"Rumors that the prince has vanished have spread throughout the court," Giles told them. "Since Holis couldn't produce the prince to refute them, he gave up, admitted it, and offered a reward for his return. He's still trying to keep the news from the populace, though I doubt that will be possible much longer. But no one's offering any money for you, girl, so if you trouble me . . ."

It was only then that his gaze fell on the sword and shield. His mouth opened and closed several times before he found his voice. "You stole them?"

If he hadn't felt so wretched, Edoran would have grinned.

Then Giles' eyes narrowed. "You really were working with your mother. I commend you, girl. I didn't believe it."

"She was not!" Edoran exclaimed.

"Believe what you like," Arisa snapped. "You have no authority over me or Edoran, and you're not taking either of us anywhere."

"But I am," said Giles. "His Highness, and the sword and shield,

are all going right back to the palace, where they belong."

Edoran couldn't have said what subtle shift in the man's expression gave him away, but suddenly he knew. "He's lying! He has no intention of taking me back."

Giles smiled. "Well, it occurs to me that there might be people who'd pay more for you than Holis would, especially with the sword and shield as part of the package. The three of you together . . . I'd be offering the whole throne of Deorthas, for sale to the highest bidder."

Arisa leaped at him, but he'd clearly been expecting it—his rapier sprang from the scabbard, swiping her blade aside. That wouldn't have mattered so much, but the hard kick to the wrist that followed it broke her grip and sent the knife spinning into the darkness.

"Bad move, girl." Giles' smile now was the one Edoran used to see when he'd angered his tutor in some small way. That smile meant a beating that would leave him sore for days, but that left no bruise he could complain about. "I have no quarrel with you," the fencing master continued, "but I have no need to keep you alive, either."

"You do if you want to sell Edoran to my mother. You need me to act as a go-between." Arisa was clutching her wrist, but her back was straight. Her plain face, in the flickering light, seemed cast in steel. "You won't even be able to contact her without me."

If she could fight on, with no weapon but her wits . . .

The idea that came to Edoran then made his blood run cold—but what choice did he have? Giles would never let him escape,

but he couldn't kill him either. The sword and shield were far less important than capturing the prince. And Arisa was of no importance at all.

If he thought about it, he might lose his nerve. And it was time Edoran rescued something!

Two swift steps took him to the horse. The sound of a rapier rasping free of its sheath made Giles turn. His eyes flickered, but he didn't look too surprised. And not at all frightened, curse him.

Though Edoran had to admit, Giles didn't have much to be frightened of.

"Take the sword and shield and run," Edoran told Arisa. "I can delay him for a few moments, at least."

Master Giles laughed.

Arisa didn't.

"What about you? I promised—"

"I release you from it," said Edoran. "Get the sword and shield away—"

Giles suddenly saw that he meant it. He turned his back on Edoran and took a step toward the gear pile, where the sword and shield lay.

Edoran ran forward, ready—absolutely ready, he promised himself—to run the sword in his hand right through Giles' back and out the other side. He was so frightened and furious that he might even have done it. He would never know, because as the sharp point neared him the fencing master spun, knocking Edoran's blade wide.

The blow was so hard, it almost jarred the hilt from his hand.

Edoran leaped back, his palm and wrist stinging. Giles followed, and he jumped back again, keeping himself just out of reach of the flashing point.

The fencing master was smiling again. That smile, and the confident step forward after Edoran's retreat, were so familiar that Edoran could feel the old pattern falling into place around them. The pattern that ended with his elbows and ribs stinging from the lash of Giles' blade, and defeat bitter in his heart. Could he break that pattern?

Arisa had said that a left-handed fighter had an advantage against a right-handed man, who wouldn't be accustomed to seeing the familiar moves from the opposite side. But a lefty would be accustomed to fighting men who were right-handed. She'd also said that trying to force someone to learn to fight with their weaker hand was iniquitous—though she hadn't phrased it that way. She'd tried to teach Edoran to fence with his left hand, and the lessons had ended in scandal and disaster . . . but it hadn't been a *fencing* disaster.

Edoran moved the sword to his left hand and had the satisfaction of seeing Master Giles' eyes narrow.

When the next blow shot toward him, he parried it. And the next. The next got through, and pain arced from his elbow. But it was his right arm, not the one that held his sword, and Edoran was accustomed to pain when he fenced with Master Giles.

To dance back, parrying and ducking, was what he'd done for years. He did it now, struggling not to trip in the tangling grass, to keep from being backed into the clutching bushes.

Soon he'd parried several score of blows. His left arm and wrist were aching from the exertion alone when Giles' rapier seemed to wrap itself around his blade like a serpent, instead of the rigid steel it was.

The fencing master yanked the sword out of Edoran's grasp and seized his collar. Shaking and sweaty, Edoran was almost glad to quit. Pain was shooting through his right arm. When he looked down, he saw that his coat sleeve bore a red splotch just above his elbow. Blood. Giles had been fighting with an edged sword, and while he hadn't exactly won . . .

Edoran looked over to the other side of the fire. The sword, the shield, and Arisa were gone.

CHAPTER 5

THE M∞NLESS NIGHT

*The Moonless Night: a person of ill intent,
without conscience or pity.*

5

He'd succeeded! For the first time since Weasel had been kid-napped, Edoran had done something right.

So why was he worse off now than he'd been before?

Giles had tied Edoran up and crashed around in the woods for almost half an hour before he'd been convinced that Arisa, and the sword and shield, were really gone. When he returned to the fire where he'd left the prince, he'd freed his feet, put Edoran up on his horse, retied his feet to the stirrups and his hands to the pommel of the saddle—and gagged him for good measure.

Edoran was a good enough rider that he considered trying to kick the horse to a gallop. If he chose a moment when Giles was distracted, the beast might be able to tear the reins from his grip. Then what? In daylight Edoran might have been able to guide the horse with his legs, and by shifting his weight in the saddle—many horses were sensitive to such cues. But they also disliked running when they couldn't see well. In the dark woods, with no hand on the reins to give clear commands, the horse probably wouldn't run far enough to make a difference. When they came out onto the moonlit main road . . .

But they never reached the road. After cutting through woods and rough fields, with much cursing, Giles finally struck the narrow track he'd been looking for—and it was both too rough and too dark for Edoran to convince the horse to bolt.

He turned his attention to the rope that bound his wrists, but there was no give in the cord, and the knots were solid. His bonds seemed to grow tighter as he struggled, and he realized his wrists were swelling and abandoned the attempt.

He had no idea where Giles was taking him, but judging by the position of the moon, which glowed in fitful patches through the bare branches, they were moving back toward the city. That made no sense to Edoran, though by now he was so tired that not much made sense to him. He finally fell into a half-waking doze, sufficiently aware to keep himself upright in the saddle, but unconscious of the passage of time. The rising sun roused him, and it was several hours after that when they finally reached the . . . place that was their destination.

Giles cut Edoran's feet free of the stirrups, then took the time to untie the cord that held his hands to the pommel, leaving Edoran's wrists still bound as he dragged him off the horse and up the steps to the front door.

The building baffled Edoran at first, for it was bigger than even a large farmhouse, but it was built too roughly, of stone and unplaned logs, to be a nobleman's manor. Only after they entered, and he saw the animal skins that served as rugs and decorated the walls, did Edoran realize that this must be some wealthy shareholder's hunting lodge. Possibly a royal lodge, for the furniture was swathed in sheets, and the air had the stuffiness of long disuse. This place certainly had a caretaker, but Giles must have gotten rid of him somehow, for the tension in his shoulders eased as soon as he pulled Edoran inside.

He left Edoran and went back out, and the prince had just roused his sleepy brain enough to wonder if he should try to run when Giles returned, carrying a length of chain and a couple of padlocks.

He dragged Edoran over to the cold hearth and fastened one end of the chain to the thick post that held up one corner of the mantel. Then he pulled off Edoran's left boot and locked the other end around Edoran's ankle, so tightly that the links dug into his flesh. Only then did he cut the cord that bound the prince's wrists, stepping back while Edoran ungagged himself.

His fingers were swollen and numb, and it took him several tries to pull down the kerchief that had been tied over his mouth and spit out the sodden rag. Edoran had thought he was afraid. He'd thought he was terrified. But the words that surged from his lips in a rasping croak were, "How dare you!"

Then he started to cough.

Giles tossed him a water flask.

If Edoran's hands hadn't been so stiff he might have caught it, and Giles sneered as he picked it up and clumsily freed the stopper. Edoran's voice sounded more normal when he continued, "You must be mad. You'll hang for this!"

"That depends on who I sell you to. Some of the Isolian dukes might pay even more than the Falcon would. Especially if I can convince them to go in on it together. But before I do that, I need more information. A lot more. You'd better make yourself comfortable, Your Highness. You're going to be here a while. In fact . . ."

He went through a door at one side of the big front room—a combination of sitting room and dining room, Edoran thought, for there were couches and chairs in front of the hearth, and a long table with chairs stacked atop it on the far side.

Edoran had to pull off his other boot to walk smoothly, and even then the chain around his ankle was too short to allow him to reach any of the furniture. There was a pile of wood beside the fireplace, but no tongs or poker. The wood itself, cut for kindling, was both too short and too light for a weapon— particularly against a swordsman of Giles' caliber.

The fencing master returned a few minutes later, carrying an armload of blankets and a covered chamber pot. He tossed the blankets to Edoran and set the pot on the other side of the hearth, within reach of the chain. "There you go, my prince. I'll be back . . . eventually."

Edoran's jaw dropped. "You're going to leave me here? Chained? You must be joking. I can't possibly—"

"You don't have a choice." The fencing master turned to go.

"Wait!" Edoran cried. "What about food?"

Giles, who had reached the door, turned to look back. "Perhaps by the time I return you'll be ready to ask for it nicely."

He went out, closing the door behind him—and the piece of wood Edoran hurled at it struck the stone wall instead, making only a dull thud the fencing master probably didn't even hear.

Edoran listened and thought he heard hoof beats, but the walls were so thick he couldn't be sure, and no one passed in front of the windows.

So had Giles just gone to stable his tired horse? Or had he really gone somewhere else? The chamber pot seemed to support the latter theory, but Edoran waited for almost half an hour before he concluded that the fencing master had abandoned him.

Giles wouldn't have left him ungagged if there was anyone near enough to hear a call for help, but Edoran shouted anyway, until his voice began to crack.

Then he pulled a blanket around himself and sat on the thick hearth rug—bearskin, by the look of it—to think. For whatever reason, Giles had no fear that the lodge's caretaker would come along and find Edoran, so there was no use hoping for that. And hunting lodges were deliberately placed as far from farms and villages as possible, so the odds of anyone passing by were very poor.

Would Arisa come for him? Probably not. Edoran had released her from her promise, and she knew that Giles would never kill him. Edoran was worth far more alive than dead, but she had no assurance that her mother's men wouldn't kill Weasel . . . so she'd rescue him first. She'd probably assume that the reason the cards had told her to take Edoran along was to help her keep the sword and shield out of Giles' hands. He'd now done that, so there was no pressing reason for her to rescue him.

Edoran felt a flash of satisfaction at the memory of Giles' fury. He could never outfight his old tutor, but he'd managed to hold him off for longer than he'd believed possible. Because he'd been fencing with his left hand? Or had Giles, too, unconsciously fallen into the old pattern, pressing attack after attack without really trying to defeat his opponent?

The cut above his elbow ached, but it had stopped bleeding toward the beginning of the ride. Now Edoran rolled up his sleeve and looked at it. Not too deep, and when he took the kerchief that had held his gag and used a bit of water from the flask to clean it, it appeared to be healing properly. He rolled his sleeve back down and looked around the room for something he could use, for either a weapon or to escape. There wasn't much.

Most of the furniture was hidden under the dust sheets, and Edoran couldn't reach it anyway. There was nothing near the fireplace except the woodpile—though he dismantled that, hoping that someone had dropped a knife down behind it. Or better yet, a pistol. Not surprisingly, no one had. There wasn't even a striker to allow him to start a fire.

In fact, there was nothing within reach except the rug, the blankets, and the chamber pot Giles had left him. Edoran used the chamber pot and then, having nothing else to do, he restacked the wood, noting that the sticks on the bottom of the pile were still green.

This confirmed his belief that someone had been caring for the place recently, but that didn't do him any good now.

Trying to think of something that would help, Edoran wrapped himself up in the blankets and sat back down on the rug. He really meant to come up with a plan, but it had been a long night. Soon he found himself lying on the rug, and a few minutes later he was asleep.

He didn't wake till the door banged against the wall. Sitting up, blinking sleep from his eyes, he saw that it was dusk—just light enough for him to recognize Giles' form in the doorway.

"Still here, I see," said the fencing master pleasantly. "Excellent."

"As you pointed out, I don't have much choice." Edoran tried to keep his voice pleasant too. If he didn't provoke the man, perhaps he wouldn't have to beg for a meal.

The fencing master looked around the room, then studied Edoran once more. When he was satisfied that all was as he'd left it, he went back outside. He didn't return for so long that Edoran began to worry, but when he came in he carried a large burlap bag and a couple of glass bottles, the kind that, in Edoran's experience, usually held rum or some other hard liquor. One of them was only partly full.

"Light first, I think," he announced, and set his burden on the table before he went to kindle the lamps. Then he came over and started a fire in the big hearth, smiling when Edoran shrank from him.

He returned to the table and laid out provisions: a big chunk of ham, wrapped in oiled paper, and loaves of bread, cheese, assorted root vegetables, and a few apples, all a bit wrinkled from their long stay in some cellar bin. Edoran felt a flash of regret for the palace glasshouse, which put fresh vegetables, and even some fruits, on his table all through the year. But this was no time to complain about the quality of the food—Master Giles was perfectly capable of responding to such complaints by refusing to give him any.

He waited in silence while Giles made sandwiches, sliced up a turnip, and set a plate with a sandwich and half the turnip down beside the prince. He also took Edoran's water flask and refilled it before eating his own meal. Edoran noted that Giles peeled his half of the turnip, but, tearing into the sandwich like a starving beggar, he had no intention of complaining. He picked up a piece of turnip in his hands and ate the flesh away from the peel. It was too strong, and woody, but by the time Edoran finished it he was full enough that he didn't want to eat the skin—and when he'd started his meal he'd been considering it!

How dare Giles starve him like that?

He dared, Edoran thought, because he planned to sell the prince to someone who'd protect him from Edoran's vengeance. But if he had nothing to fear from Edoran or Holis, then why was he drinking so much?

Watching the fencing master consume only half a sandwich, while he downed most of the remainder of the bottle, Edoran decided that he'd eaten earlier . . . and started drinking before he'd arrived here as well. He didn't have a lot of experience with drunks. When one of his courtiers drank too much, his friends usually removed him from the royal presence before he could make a fool of himself. But he'd seen more than a few men in the early stages of inebriety, and one of the first things drink did was make them loose-tongued. So . . .

"Did you find the information you were looking for?" Edoran kept his voice light—just making conversation. It seemed to work, for Giles laughed abruptly.

"No. And yes. Which means Holis isn't as smart as he thinks he is."

Edoran frowned, wondering if Giles was more drunk than he appeared, but the fencing master went on, "He finally figured out that your valet was selling the information that you'd run to . . . well, anyone who paid him for it. He's clapped up in a cell now, but that just makes the others more eager t' gossip. With an old friend, at least."

Was Giles' voice slurring, just a bit?

"Was that how you found out about my disappearance so quickly? How clever of you."

The admiring tone was evidently too much, even through Giles' alcoholic fog, for he cast Edoran a suspicious glance. "They're all talking now," he said. "Every servant down to the stable boys, 'cept those personally loyal to Holis. And why not? The rumor of your disappearance is beginning to spread through the city now. The amount of the reward grows with every retelling, too, but it's still not as much as I can prob'ly get . . . elsewhere."

For a man looking forward to acquiring a fortune, he didn't sound very happy, and Edoran was seized with sudden insight. "You're afraid they'll catch you before you can get away with the money. That's why you're drinking so much. Because you know a hanged man can't spend it!"

He'd forgotten how quickly the fencing master moved. Even

half-drunk, Giles had risen from the table and crossed the floor before Edoran struggled onto his knees. He threw up his hands to protect his face, but Giles swept them aside with his left hand and struck with his right.

The blow knocked Edoran to the floor, and bright bubbles obscured his vision. Through the ringing in his ears he heard Giles' footsteps retreat, the scrape of his chair, the clink of bottle on glass.

He should have expected it. Giles was mean enough sober— he was bound to be a violent drunk.

When his head cleared, Edoran sat up again and gingerly felt the left side of his face. Giles' blow had landed on top of the bruises the robbers had left him, and the flesh around his eye was beginning to swell. It certainly hurt.

Edoran dampened his kerchief with water and held it against his face. Giles might not be free to kill him, but he could still hurt Edoran in a dozen different ways. He had inflicted enough pain on the prince, even in the days when he hadn't dared to leave a mark on him . . . and those days were clearly over.

If there was something else he'd needed to learn, Edoran might have risked it. But since he couldn't think of any question that would help him, he kept his mouth shut, watching as Giles sent the level of liquor in the bottle down and down.

He almost finished it, and there was a lurch in his smooth movements when he finally rose to his feet. "Keep the fire going, boy." He walked slowly over to a couch, one that stood well out of Edoran's limited reach, and pulled off the dust cover. He contemplated it for a moment, then went to the messy pile of blankets Edoran had abandoned as the fire grew warmer. He took two of the three of them and smiled.

Edoran held hard to his resolution not to cringe, but Giles' gaze was oddly unfocused. "On'y one blanket, you'll have to keep it going." The fencing master chuckled and turned back to his couch. "Use th' wood on top," he added. "On the bottom's all green."

He lay down, wrapping himself in blankets and dust sheet all together. Within moments his breathing settled into the rhythms of sleep.

Edoran watched him glumly. Chained to the hearth, with all this wood available, he would hardly freeze. On the other hand, he was no closer to escape with Giles drunk than he'd been with him sober—or gone.

Was there any chance he could throw a piece of firewood hard and straight enough to knock Giles unconscious? He'd missed the door earlier, and it was a much larger target than a man's head, half buried in blankets. But Giles was unconscious now, and it wasn't doing Edoran any good. Even if he managed to hit the man, all he'd accomplish would be that Giles would wake with an even worse headache than his hangover would already supply. And if by some miracle Edoran struck hard enough to kill, the fencing master's corpse would then keep him company while he starved to death.

In sight of food, too. A lot of food. Edoran eyed the supplies Giles had brought—enough to keep both him and the fencing master for several days, perhaps a week. But not, Edoran thought, enough to feed him while Giles rode to the Isolian border, made his deal, and returned. So Edoran had no way to know what the man planned to do next—and even if Giles left him alone, that still wouldn't allow him to escape.

Finally Edoran decided to put the green wood on the fire. He didn't know what it would do, but there had to be some reason Giles had told him not to.

In a burst of optimism he stacked a huge mound of green sticks on the fire . . . which soon started to go out. Edoran had only one blanket. He scorched his fingers pulling them out again, built up the fire with dry wood, and then set a few green pieces on top, by way of a controlled experiment.

They didn't do much. They were slower to catch fire, and when they did burn they produced more smoke, and more crackling pops, but that was all.

On the other hand . . . If they made enough smoke, might some distant neighbor think the lodge was on fire and come to investigate?

Edoran hesitated. That would probably work better in the daylight, but in the day he might not be allowed to build a fire. It was dark now, but still early, and the moon was almost full. Try!

This time Edoran built his fire carefully, taking pains to keep it going as he added more and more green timber. Soon smoke poured up the chimney, sometimes puffing into the room as well, but it didn't look like enough to Edoran. He thought it over and soaked one corner of his blanket. Then he wrapped it around the longest stick in the pile and held it over the blaze. It soon began to steam in a most satisfactory fashion . . . and if Edoran didn't pull it out in time, he might have more fire than he wanted!

But he could smother the flames in the rug if he had to. Surely it could steam for a few more—

The door opened. Edoran heard the soft *snick* of the latch and spun, opening his mouth to shout for help, but the man who stood in the doorway raised a finger to his lips.

His hair, pulled back in an untidy queue at the nape of his neck, was almost all gray, and his face was lined, but he crept into the room with an ease that reminded Edoran of the way Arisa moved when she wanted to be quiet.

His eyes roamed over the lamp-lit room, taking in the chained prince, the sleeping fencing master, and the food on the table. He stepped over to the table and picked up the nearly empty bottle, sniffed it, and grinned.

Edoran couldn't wait any longer. "Get me out of this!" he whispered. "Please! There's a re—"

The man gestured for silence once more, his gaze on Master Giles. The laugh lines around his eyes deepened, and Edoran had to agree that the fencing master had earned his fate. Only then did the man walk silently over to Edoran.

"Where's the key?" His soft murmur was quieter than Edoran's whisper, and he'd gone straight to the point. Edoran approved. Unfortunately, he didn't know.

"Giles put it in his pocket yesterday," he murmured back. "But I don't know if he put it somewhere else since."

The man's shaggy brows rose in appalled astonishment. "You've been chained here all day?"

Edoran nodded. "Can't you pick the lock or something?"

The stranger snorted. "Not everyone is like your friend. In fact, very few are. A good thing, too."

His friend? How did this man know about Weasel? Did he know who Edoran was?

The stranger showed no sign of the deference most people displayed on meeting the prince, bowing only to examine the lock that secured Edoran's ankle, and frowning at the way the links bit into his flesh. He looked at the identical lock that fastened the chain around the post, grimaced, and then crept across to the sleeping fencing master.

Edoran watched as the man went slowly through Giles' pockets. The fencing master was drunk, but anyone might be awakened by hands on their body.

The stranger might not be a pickpocket like Weasel, but his touch was light. He went for the easier targets first, searching the big pockets in the skirts of Giles' coat, then the small pocket on the front of his vest. He appeared to be holding his breath as he eased his hand into the pocket of Giles' britches, and Edoran held his breath too.

The fencing master stirred and wiggled deeper into the cushions, but he didn't wake.

The stranger—who was he, anyway, and how had he come here?—pulled his hand free. It was empty. He stared down at the sleeping man, then turned to Edoran and lifted one hand, then the other. His expression proclaimed that the gesture was a question, but it took two repetitions before Edoran got it.

The prince pointed to Giles, then slowly raised his right hand. The fencing master was right-handed . . . and he was sleeping on his right side, making the right britches pocket—the pocket in which a right-handed man was most likely to keep keys—unreachable.

Edoran pantomimed striking a sleeping man on the head—with a piece of firewood, say.

The stranger shook his head and drifted out of the room, through the door that led to the rest of the house. He returned a few minutes later, carrying not a good blunt instrument, or the biggest knife in the kitchen, but, of all things, a long feather.

He tiptoed back to the couch, lowered himself to his knees, and began tickling the fencing master's nose.

The nose wrinkled, and a muscle in Giles' cheek twitched. The tip of the feather darted and danced, and Edoran scowled. Bashing Giles over the head would be less risky—and more likely to succeed.

But the stranger persisted, and suddenly Giles sneezed.

The stranger dropped instantly to the floor and slithered under the couch, just as Giles' eyes blinked open.

His gaze went first to Edoran, who suddenly realized that he should probably be faking sleep, but it was too late now. He stared at the two men, one under the couch and one atop it, both of them looking at him. A giggle rose in his throat, but terror suppressed it.

Seeing the prince chained where he'd left him seemed to reassure the fencing master. He looked around the room and found nothing amiss. He reached up to rub his cheek, then rolled onto his left side, pulling the blankets around him once more.

The stranger seemed not even to be breathing, but his gaze was fixed on the prince's face. He waited till Edoran signaled that the fencing master was asleep before dragging himself out and sliding his hand carefully under the blankets. Edoran saw his shoulders stiffen, and he knew, even before the man's hand emerged, that the keys had been found.

Fighting down surges of fear and impatience, Edoran kept still as the man crept back to him. The click of the opening lock sounded horribly loud in the stillness, and they both froze. The fencing master's steady breathing never faltered.

A hand under his elbow helped Edoran to his feet, and his knees were so wobbly he was grateful for it. Every muscle in his body screamed for him to run, but he picked up his boots and forced himself to creep quietly after the stranger—who was he?—to the door.

He'd left it ajar so the latch didn't click, and the lodge's absent caretaker had oiled the hinges. The door swung open without a sound, and Edoran stepped out into the night. The cold air was as refreshing as water on his sweaty skin. He hurried quietly off the porch, almost tripping on the steps in his haste.

There was a stocky dark horse tied to the rail at one side of the yard. Edoran had his boots on and the reins untied by the time the stranger had eased the door shut and come over to join him. He mounted, then reached down to lift Edoran up behind him.

Edoran clutched the saddle's hard rim. The horse's rump rolled more than a saddle would, but he still wanted the rider to kick the beast into a gallop—to run and run into the night.

Of course, if he did, the sound of galloping hoof beats might rouse Giles, who might still catch up with them. Not to mention the risk of a fall, galloping in the dark. If they sneaked away while the fencing master slept the night through, he'd never be able to find them. So it made sense that the man was only walking his horse down the shadowed track. Still . . .

"Why didn't you bash him on the head?" Edoran kept his voice low, though they were far enough from the lodge that a normal voice probably wouldn't have carried. "We could have taken him prisoner. Chained him up!"

He could only see the back of the stranger's head, but he had a feeling the man was smiling.

"It's difficult to hit a man on the head hard enough to knock him out without killing him," the stranger replied. His voice was louder than Edoran's, and the prince found his spirits rising.

"Most of the time," the stranger went on, "when people try to knock someone unconscious they either kill them, or they strike so softly they just make their victim angry. And I'd hate to do that."

"He was drunk," said Edoran. "You could have handled him."

"Even drunk, he's still the best swordsman in Deorthas," said the stranger. "And I'm . . . not. No, thank you."

He'd started to say something that he was, and Edoran wondered why he'd changed his mind. But if his rescuer wanted to keep his privacy, Edoran owed him that. And a lot more besides. He sighed.

"What?" the stranger asked.

"This is the second time in a week someone's had to rescue me. I really am hopelessly incompetent."

"Oh, I don't know," said the stranger. "If Your Highness hadn't sent up that smoke signal, I'd have passed right by the lodge. You can't see it from the track. And if your Master Giles had been awake and sober . . . well, this could have gone much less smoothly. So don't be too hard on yourself."

Your Highness. He did know who Edoran was. He'd known who Master Giles was too, and he sounded as if he'd been *looking* for the lodge.

"Who are you?" Edoran demanded.

CHAPTER 6

THE STAR

The Star: holiness. Aspiration to the divine. All gods.

6

"My name's Sandeman," said the stranger. "And I'm the man who'll be taking you back to the palace."

"I can't go," said Edoran. "Not yet. Not until Weasel can come too. And if you know Weasel, you know that he's worth several of me. Three at least!"

The stranger laughed. "I don't disagree about young Weasel's worth. Perhaps. But lad, you're worth every bit as much, just for yourself. And even leaving aside your personal worth, we can't afford to lose the heir to Deorthas' throne—to the Falcon, or in any other way. She may have convinced herself that she can let you live, but as long as any king of the true line remains, she'll face rebellion after rebellion. Sooner or later she'll be forced to kill you. And even that won't end it. If one person can seize the throne by force of arms, so can another. You may not be ready to . . . ah, take up the burden of kingship, but you're the only alternative to endless war between the two religious and economic factions in the realm. Weasel is important, that I grant you. But your own safety is absolutely vital. Which is why you're going straight back to the palace. I'm sorry," he added. "But there it is."

Edoran already knew all of that, but . . . "How do you know so much about Weasel? Are you a friend of Justice Holis'?" The man was plainly, almost roughly, dressed, but his speech was educated, with only a trace of a country accent.

"No, I've never met the justice," said Sandeman. "And I only met your young friend once. Though I have to say, it was memorable."

He didn't know Holis, but he'd met Weasel. Met him just once, under memorable circumstances. And most people thought of the tension between the townsmen and the country folk of Deorthas as being only economic. Many people weren't even aware that there were—or had once been—two religions.

"You're the leader of the Hidden faith, aren't you?" Edoran asked. "The one who had Weasel kidnapped that night, and wore a mask and cloak when you talked with him."

Weasel had discussed that meeting with Edoran several times. "The calm-voiced man" was how he'd identified his chief captor.

Sandeman's voice wasn't calm now. "How in Dialan's name . . . ?" He took a deep breath, and then another. "I've heard rumors that you weren't very bright. Which certainly confirms my doubts about listening to rumors! How did you figure that out?"

"Weasel described you pretty well," Edoran told him.

"Weasel never saw me! He had more sense than to try."

The Hidden faith had been illegal in Deorthas for the past three centuries. Could he use the fact that Sandeman was a Hidden priest to force the man to let him go? He could. *If you take me back, I'll turn you in.* It would be that simple, but there was something about this man that made him hesitate.

"Smart lad," said Sandeman. "I'd have tied you up in a shed somewhere, told the town guard where to find you, and then run."

"How did you know what I was thinking?"

"It was an obvious possibility, once you knew who I was. But even if I let you go, every guardsman in the realm is looking for you. And far too many people know about the reward. You'd never make it, lad."

"But I don't look like a prince," Edoran objected.

A soft laugh shook the man in front of him. "You certainly don't! But the moment you open your mouth, that accent . . . It's not just city, it's high-noble city. If you could purchase food and shelter without speaking to anyone, you might have a chance. But they might be suspicious of a mute boy who answered the description of the missing prince, don't you think?"

"Wonderful," Edoran muttered. If he couldn't travel on his own, or make Sandeman help him, how could he find the Falcon and Weasel? If he could catch up with Arisa, she could do the talking—and tell some lie that would keep people from suspecting him too. But he had no clue how to find Arisa. In fact . . .

"How did you find me?" he asked.

"I was . . . consulting with a friend," Sandeman told him. "And we happened to catch sight of Master Giles, who was in the midst of an intense conversation with one of the palace servants. Holis had already clapped your loose-tongued valet into a cell, but my friend knew Giles' history. She found it surprising that anyone from the palace would be talking to him. She said Justice Holis had ordered all your old tutors out of the city, and she found his mere presence there suspicious."

"It wasn't an order," said Edoran. "But it was a pretty strong hint. Almost a threat. So you followed him?"

"To make a long story short, yes."

Edoran frowned. "What were you doing in the city in the first place? Weasel met you in some town to the *west* of the city. And how did you find out about Giles and my other tutors? That's not common knowledge."

"I have ways," Sandeman said calmly. "You should be grateful—"

It all fell into place then.

"You have a spy in the palace!" Edoran exclaimed. "You're the Hidden leader—you heard I was missing, or she sent word to you, and you came to the city to talk to your palace spy about it."

Sandeman sighed. "I'll never believe any rumor, ever again. I swear it."

"Don't worry about it," Edoran told him. "I think every servant in the palace is somebody's spy. You said *she*. . . . Hmm. I bet it's that seamstress who got Arisa and me out of the closet. I should have wondered about that at the time."

"I'm not going to name my friend," said Sandeman. "Nor confirm that she works in the palace. She wouldn't have to, you know. All she'd need is a connection with someone who does work there and would pass on gossip. It's dangerous for a Hidden teacher to live in the city, let alone in the palace itself."

That was true. The townsmen, led by the church of the One God, believed that the followers of the Hidden faith sacrificed children. One of the Hidden had been stoned to death by a mob when Edoran was young. He hadn't heard about it at the time, but his father had written about the incident in his journals. The king had added that there was no evidence that the followers of the Hidden faith had ever sacrificed anyone except King Deor. That was more than a thousand years ago, and Deor's sacrifice had been voluntary, according to the legend. But with the church of the One God preaching against the Hidden, that seamstress was taking an appalling risk.

"Why do you keep a spy in the palace?" Edoran asked. "What good does it do you?"

"Our lives depend on the king not deciding to actively persecute our faith," Sandeman told him. "The years when King Regalis and his minions hanged all our teachers weren't so very long ago."

"They were hanged because they raised rebellion against the king," said Edoran. "Not because of their faith." At least, that was what his father had written.

"But it was their faith that revealed to them how disastrous the king's policy would be," said Sandeman. "So it comes down to the same thing, doesn't it?"

Edoran thought this over. "I don't think so. Not exactly. And no king has tried to get rid of you since then, whatever the One God's priests may have done. So it seems to me that putting a spy into the palace is a big risk for very little gain . . . unless . . . Oh, rot. It's the earthquakes, isn't it? You think those earthquakes that happened when I was born were a portent, just like all the One God priests. Just like every senile hag with a deck of cards."

"We have good reason to want to know what the government is planning," Sandeman told him.

Edoran snorted. "Did you spy on my father?"

"Well . . . no."

"That's what I thought. So, do you think those quakes mean I'm going to save the realm or destroy it? Or some other weird thing?"

Saving or destroying the realm were the most popular theories, but Edoran had heard others. That he would be able to sense gold in the depths of the earth, like a diviner could sense water, was one of his favorites.

Sandeman sighed. "We *hope* it's a portent that you'll be the king we've been waiting for. But I'm afraid all three of you still have a long way to go."

All three of him? "You're even crazier than the hags with cards."

"Why do you hate the arcanara cards so much?" Sandeman asked.

"What, your spy didn't tell you?" Edoran was tired of being spied on. Tired of all of it. Weasel was the only person he'd really been able to trust. If he couldn't get him back . . . Edoran shivered.

"She never found out," Sandeman admitted.

"It doesn't matter," Edoran said wearily. "No one paid any attention to my order not to use them, anyway."

Just like every other order he'd ever given.

They rode on in silence.

It was still several hours short of dawn when Sandeman decided to make camp. "Master Giles will probably sleep late, considering what he drank. And since he has no way of knowing how you escaped or where you went afterward, we might as well get some sleep ourselves."

Edoran, climbing stiffly down from the horse, was ready for a rest. It was harder to find dry wood in the dark, but he finally returned to camp with a decent armload, and Sandeman made a fire.

"Your last cold night, Your Highness. If we get an early start, we should reach the palace tomorrow afternoon."

Edoran sighed. "It took me four days to walk this far."

"That's why men ride horses."

Edoran had been thinking. "You've got a deck of arcanara cards, right?"

It had worked with Arisa, after all.

"I'm the old gods' spokesman on this earth," Sandeman said comfortably. "The cards are how they communicate with people who have the withe to channel their power. Of course I have a deck."

"So if you laid out the cards, and they told you not to take me back, you'd have to do it? Being the old gods' servant, and all that."

"I'm their spokesman, not their slave," said Sandeman dryly. "But if they warned me that taking you back was a bad idea, I'd certainly think twice."

"Then do it," said Edoran. "Ask if you should take me back and lay out the cards. And if disaster threatens, and there's nothing to rely on, then will you help me go on? And find Weasel, and get him out of the Falcon's hands alive?"

Sandeman eyed him thoughtfully. "I'm not going to promise anything, no matter what the cards say. But I'll lay them out on one condition—you tell me why you hate them."

He settled back to wait, with the air of a man who had all the time in the world.

It was embarrassing, but why not? He didn't have to tell Sandeman all of it, anyway.

"The fool always shows up as my significator," Edoran said. "Everyone laughs at me."

Sandeman waited, but he said nothing more. The fact that chaos and the tower always followed the fool, and the terror those cards had evoked in him, before he even understood what they signified, were things he'd never confided to anyone—and he saw no reason to start now.

The Hidden priest sighed. "I can understand why you'd feel that way, especially with all your tutors working to make you look stupid. But if that's really your answer, then you're not the king we need, whatever the portents might say. Oh, all right."

He didn't have to dig into his saddlebags for the deck—he kept it in his pocket.

Edoran bit back a smile. When the question of taking Edoran back was answered with the worst threat imaginable, this man would listen to his gods.

Sandeman spread a blanket on the ground, shuffled the deck three times, and handed it to Edoran. "This is about your life more than mine. Ask the question that's in your heart."

As he shuffled, Edoran tried to will the cards to keep him from the palace, but he wasn't really concerned. No matter what he was thinking about, the fool, chaos, and the tower always came up.

He handed the deck back to Sandeman, who turned the top card and looked at it. His brows rose.

"This card represents you."

He laid the lord on the blanket between them. Edoran stared at the richly dressed man, who stood with one hand holding a staff and the other resting on a globe.

"That's not me. I'm *always* the fool."

"The fool isn't a fool, you know," said Sandeman gently. "He represents wisdom of the heart. As people change, their significators change too. Someone who started as the fool might well grow into this card, for this represents a man of intelligence, good judgment, and peace."

Edoran gasped. "That's my father!"

Sandeman sat up straighter. "Was that your question? You wanted to know if he was murdered?"

Edoran hadn't been thinking of anything in particular, but that question had been in his heart since the day of his father's death. So much so that Sandeman's palace spy had reported it to him, Edoran noted.

"Go on."

Sandeman frowned. "Are you certain you want—"

Edoran clutched the man's wrist. "Go on!"

Sandeman sighed. "I suppose you have a right to know, even now."

Edoran didn't release his grip. The question in his heart wasn't whether his father had been murdered, or even who killed him—he'd known both those things from the moment his nurse had come, weeping, into his playroom.

All he needed to know was *how* it had been done. How it had been done so cleverly that even honest investigators said the king's death was an accident, and Edoran had never been able to convince anyone otherwise.

"Lay the next card," he commanded.

Sandeman did so. "This supports you. Or rather, this supported the king."

Cloaked in black, the traitor looked over the smoldering ruin he had created. The man on the card looked nothing like Pettibone, but the aura, the presence of his old regent, filled Edoran's memory when he looked at it. He shivered.

Sandeman was watching him, concerned. "It's Regent Pettibone, isn't it? Just as you claimed."

Edoran had burst into tears as a five-year-old when he tried to explain to the people around him that *that man* had killed his father. He'd usually been screaming by the end of the tale, hysterical, because no one ever listened and he *knew* it was true. It hadn't helped that he couldn't explain how he knew. It also hadn't increased his credibility that he'd been under the impression that the master of the household, who commanded the footmen and other servants, outranked the lord commander of the army. And neither of them had believed him.

"Lay the threat," he told Sandeman.

"In its turn." Sandeman sighed. "This inspires the king."

He set the six of stars above the lord.

"Trust," Sandeman murmured. "Faith in the basic goodness of mankind."

Tears pricked Edoran's eyes. "He had that."

"And this threatens him," Sandeman went on.

The nine of fires, untimely death, fell to the lord's far left, but Edoran hardly saw the coffin pictured on the card. A flashing vision filled his mind, the vision of a horse's hooves pounding the earth, lifting for a jump. He gasped and let go of Sandeman's wrist. The vision vanished.

The Hidden priest had paled. "Your father died in a riding accident, didn't he?"

"It was no accident," Edoran said fiercely. And for the first time in his life, to this man who believed in his cards, he might be able to prove it. "Go on."

As Sandeman reached for the deck, Edoran touched his wrist once more. The priest frowned at him, but he didn't shake off Edoran's hand.

"This might have protected him," he said softly.

The fish. He'd had some opportunity, Edoran realized, and missed it. A man's voice, a stranger's, murmured in the back of his mind, I *don't trust that man, Highness. You should investigate.* . . .

Edoran recognized his father's laugh.

It was such a small slip of thought that he might have taken it for some long-forgotten memory . . . but judging by his grim expression, Sandeman had heard it too. Did Sandeman always have visions when he laid the cards, and Edoran was somehow sharing them? Or was this coming to Edoran because it was his question? Nothing like this had ever happened before.

He tightened his grip on the priest's wrist. "What next?"

"This misled him," Sandeman said. The eight of waters fell to the lord's far right. "Solitude," the priest murmured. "A time of aloneness, and need for aid."

Edoran did remember his father coming to tuck him in after his mother had died, the sense of aching grief he'd felt when his father touched him. It was an unusually vivid memory, but it was something he'd known.

Could Sandeman somehow remember it too?

"This guides you true." The priest laid down the final card, the two of waters. The card was discovery, but the vision that filled Edoran's mind was of a hoe, churning clay and water into mud, and then raking a layer of sod back over the top of the puddle. His hand clenched Sandeman's wrist so hard the man winced. Edoran let him go. He wrapped his arms around himself, trying to stop shaking.

Sandeman was frowning. "I knew the king died in a riding accident. I never heard that anyone questioned it. Not even a rumor of suspicion."

"I always knew," said Edoran. "I knew Pettibone had him killed. They examined the horse's tack, and its hooves, and even tested its feed for poison. They never thought to examine the mud it slipped in. I *knew*. But I couldn't prove it. I couldn't even figure out how."

Now he knew that as well. The shivers were abating. He still couldn't prove it. Did he need to? Pettibone was already dead. The king was dead, and proving he'd been murdered wouldn't bring him back. Still . . .

"Thank you," said Edoran. "I needed to know that. To know how it happened. To know . . ." To know that his certainty had been right. That he wasn't crazy. "Well, to know. So I thank you."

Sandeman's face, in the firelight, was troubled. Had he seen the same visions Edoran had? Or something different, that spoke specifically to him? The old gods had clearly granted their spokesman an amazing amount of withe.

"I suppose that answers my question too," Sandeman said. He didn't sound happy about it.

"Your question?" Edoran frowned. "Oh, you mean about taking me back."

He'd almost forgotten about that, but Sandeman nodded.

"I can't take you back to the palace. If the old regent could murder a king and get away with it, then it's not safe for you, either. Holis may have taken over the government, but most of the servants are still Pettibone's people, aren't they?"

"They are," Edoran confirmed. "They all detest me too."

Of course, that had been mutual. Now that he knew how his father had died, could he at least eliminate the maidservants from his suspicions? The hands on that hoe had been a man's. But that was a problem for the future. For the present . . .

"Will you help me look for the Falcon then? Help me rescue Weasel?"

"I'll look for the Falcon," Sandeman told him. "And I'll either find some way to get Weasel away from her, or I'll bring you there to negotiate for his release. When there's an army present, to keep you out of her hands!"

Edoran thought this over. He wanted to go after Weasel himself! But with every guardsman and villain in the realm looking for him . . . Sandeman and Arisa were right. At best he'd get in their way, and at worst they'd have to waste even more time rescuing him. And Weasel might not have time to spare.

He had to admit he was relieved at not having to confront the Falcon alone. Arisa could be crazy and bossy, but her mother was downright frightening. He was tired, and bruised, and dirty. He wasn't cut out for wandering around the countryside on his own, much less for heroic rescues.

"All right," said Edoran. "I'll stay somewhere safe till you need me to negotiate. But I'm holding you to that part!"

Sandeman nodded gravely. "If it looks like the Falcon is going to be captured, I'll do all I can to get you there in time."

The words had the ring of an oath, and Edoran nodded acceptance. Previously, Sandeman had refused to make promises he wasn't prepared to keep. "Very well. Where will you take me?"

Some shareholder's country mansion would be nice, but even the home of a wealthy merchant might be acceptable. Edoran could all but feel the water of a hot bath covering his aching body.

"Hmm. Yes. I think that would be as safe as anywhere you could go. Certainly no one would look for you there. And it's closer than the palace, though in the opposite direction. Yes, Caerfalas it is."

"What's Caerfalas?" Edoran asked. Many of the larger country houses had names.

Sandeman smiled. "It's a fishing village, just a bit down the coast."

Edoran's jaw dropped. "A *fishing village?*"

CHAPTER 7

THE EIGHT OF WATERS

The Eight of Waters: solitude.
A time of aloneness. The need for aid.

7

Sandeman said they should keep off the main road because that was where Giles was most likely to look for them. They plodded down the back roads, passing farms and going through this tiny village or that one. Edoran eyed the houses skeptically. They weren't dirty, exactly, but none of them were large enough to have even a proper guest room, much less a suite.

The place they stopped for lunch was a decent-size town, which held several larger buildings, including both a town hall and an inn. There was even a statue of one of the old kings, with two courtiers holding the sword and shield for him, in the central square.

Sandeman told Edoran to wait there while he purchased lunch, so Edoran watched the peasants pass back and forth, smiling and nodding at one another. The men usually wore kerchiefs around their necks, instead of lace cravats, and the women wore the same kerchiefs covering their hair. But a few men were better dressed, in tailored coats and vests.

Sometimes the peasants smiled and nodded at him, and since he didn't dare speak to anyone, he turned his gaze to the statue. He didn't know which king this was, though if he knew the date the town was founded, that might have told him. Two men were holding the sword and shield here, though in some of the old statues a woman held the shield, or even, on rare occasions, the sword.

Edoran was smiling cynically when Sandeman returned.

"What's amusing you?" The Hidden priest set out a couple of hot pastries, biscuits and jam, and a pot of pickled cabbage. It was the best meal Edoran had seen since he'd left the palace, and his mouth watered.

"I was wondering what they'd done to get themselves sculpted there." Edoran took a bite of the pastry. It tasted even better than it smelled.

"What they'd done? One of them was king."

"I know that," Edoran mumbled around a full mouth, and then swallowed. "But after we found the sword and shield, some of the courtiers began talking about those statues. They said the people who were granted the honor of holding the sword and shield for the king were his favorites, and they were speculating about what they'd have to do—or pay—to get themselves up there. So I wondered what those two did to earn it."

Sandeman was gazing at the statue now. "I suppose that's one way to look at it."

"What do you mean?" Edoran asked.

The thoughtful eyes turned to him. "What do you know about the history of the sword and shield?"

Edoran shrugged and swallowed another mouthful. "The same things everyone knows. According to the legend, there was a terrible drought or something, and Deor, who had united the warring chiefs to become the first real king we ever had, offered his life in sacrifice to the old gods if they'd end it. And they took him up on the offer."

He suddenly realized that he was talking to the head of the church that had accepted that sacrifice, and put down his pastry.

"They hung him upside down and cut his throat," Edoran went on, more carefully now. "His blood spilled into the earth and the drought—or whatever it was—ended. But his heir, King Brend, was lonely and grieved for his father, so the gods offered him the crown of earth, the sword of waters, and the shield of stars to ease his burden.

"And the legend says they did," Edoran finished. "Though I can't see how any of those things could make him less lonely. The crown was lost, but the sword and shield survived as symbols of the gods' favor to the king and the land, until Regalis lost them, too. And now Weasel and Arisa have found them again. Some people think that's a portent too," he added. "Though no one's willing to say what it's a portent of. But you might actually know. . . . Is any of that old legend about King Deor true? Was he really willing . . . I mean, ah . . . Did he really die like that?"

"Yes." Sandeman's voice was soft; his gaze returned to the statue of Deor's descendant. "Our teachers' memories of that time are more detailed than the legend most people know, but that part's true enough. They say the first teacher wept as he wielded the blade, but Deor had willingly offered his own life, that the crown of earth might come to his descendants. He never bore it himself, you know. It went directly to Brend upon his father's death."

"What did the crown look like?" Edoran asked. "The sword and shield are in the oldest portraits, but there was never a picture of any particular crown."

Sandeman smiled. "No one has a picture of the crown of earth, Highness. Your version of the rest of the story is fairly accurate, except that the gods didn't actually give Brend the sword and shield; they gave him the ability to recognize them when he found them. I'm surprised you know that much. The fisherfolk have forgotten less of our teaching than the farm folk have, but the townsmen remember almost nothing of the old truths."

It was Edoran's father who'd told him about the old legends and taught him where to look for the secret pattern of stars, hidden in the shield's embossing, and the distinctive ripple in the water pattern on the sword. He'd described them so well, and so often, that when the true sword and shield had been recovered, Edoran had been able to identify them instantly. And they hadn't done a thing for his loneliness. Though Weasel had become his friend soon after that, and Arisa had started to do the same, so he hardly cared what happened to the sword and shield. If Arisa could trade them for Weasel's freedom, Edoran would wish them good riddance.

"How long do you think it will take to locate the Falcon?" he asked.

"How could I possibly know that," Sandeman replied, "considering that I have no idea where she is? But the sooner I get you settled, the sooner I can start looking."

That was sufficient motivation for Edoran to bolt down the rest of his meal, and they set off again.

Roughly two hours after they left the town, Edoran started to smell the sea—a fresher version of it, here in the countryside. They turned onto a track that paralleled the coast, and in the gaps in the brush and dunes Edoran caught glimpses of sparkling waves, and sometimes the beach with its crashing surf. He began to hope that Caerfalas might not be so bad, but when they finally reached it, the fishing village was the most wretched huddle of huts he'd ever seen in his life.

The streets were a sea of mud, not even paved with cobblestones, much less brick. The houses—not one of them more than two or three rooms!—were made up of weathered gray boards, and even the thatch that topped them was a dirty gray-brown.

Edoran eyed those roofs uneasily. Hadn't someone told him that mice, and even rats, lived in thatched roofs?

Several people called out and waved to Sandeman, their voices barely audible over the crash of the breakers. The beach was visible from the main street—the only street, Edoran corrected himself. There were boats pulled up on the sand and men working around them. The men wore drab, dirty-looking sweaters over their britches and shirts, as the poorer sailors in the city sometimes did; they looked as shaggy and anonymous as sheep to city eyes.

The man who stomped through the mud toward them now looked even more like a sheep, Edoran thought. He had pale, curly hair and blunt features, the kind of face Edoran had always thought made people look stupid, but this man didn't look stupid.

And after the way his tutors had convinced everyone he was an idiot, maybe he shouldn't be so quick to judge.

"Sandy!" The blunt-faced man held out his hand. "It's been a long time."

His accent wasn't as country-rough as Edoran had expected. Or perhaps his ear was growing accustomed to it.

"Too long," Sandeman agreed, as the two men clasped hands. "Togger, this is Ron. He's my cousin's boy. The cousin who moved to the city to scout for us."

Togger's brows shot up, almost touching his hair. "That was a bit of a risk!"

"Too much risk, as it turned out," Sandeman said. "He got out in time, but only barely. Can you hide young Ron till my cousin can establish himself somewhere else and send for him?"

The implications of this speech set Edoran's mind reeling. Were all the people in this village of the Hidden faith? He'd been taught it had nearly died out! Would he have to pretend to be of the Hidden faith too? He didn't even know who the old gods were, much less how they were worshipped.

"Ah . . ." His voice trailed off. How could he phrase his objections without giving himself away?

Sandeman shot him an amused glance.

"Don't worry, lad. Not all here follow our faith, those who do are discreet about it, and no one will care either way. It's not like the city. You'll have no trouble here."

"I like the city," Edoran protested.

Togger eyed him askance, but Sandeman laughed.

"He was raised in the city for most of his life," he told the fisherman. "This is going to be a bit of a shock for him, but he'll probably survive. I want you to pass him off as one of your own. Better yet, take him out on the boats—that'll keep him safe from any inquiry."

"They're hunting him?" Togger asked. His expression, turned on Edoran, was softer now. "He doesn't look like a working lad. Can he even swim?"

"I certainly can," Edoran told him. What did the man mean, he didn't look like a working lad? He was as dirty as anyone here— dirtier than most!

"My cousin's a merchant," said Sandeman. "That's what the lad was training for."

Togger sighed. "He'll have to keep his mouth shut if a search comes through. That accent never came from around here."

"So you'll keep him?" Sandeman asked.

"Oh, aye," said Togger. "We owe you that much. But only men go out with the boats."

"He's fifteen," said Sandeman.

"Huh. He's small for it. Well, we'll see. Grab your gear, lad, and I'll take you to Moll's and get you settled."

"I don't have any gear," said Edoran. For the first time since he'd been robbed, that lack of possessions embarrassed him.

Togger cast him a sympathetic glance. "Had to leave in a real rush, I see. Don't worry, Moll will find something that will fit you—something sturdier than those rags!"

Sandeman nodded, so Edoran slid down from the horse's rump.

He felt utterly deserted, but Sandeman leaned down to lay a hand on his shoulder. "I'll be back as soon as I find something." The hand tightened in promise and then let go.

He was going after Weasel. Edoran stood in silence as the Hidden priest rode away. The man was doing what he wanted, so he could hardly whine about it.

Another warm hand descended on his shoulder. "He'll be back for you, lad," Togger assured him. "The teacher never breaks his word."

Teacher? Edoran almost said it aloud, but just in time he remembered that Sandeman had referred to the Hidden priests that Regalis had executed as "teachers." Pretending to be of the Hidden faith was going to be harder than Sandeman had assumed.

"Who's this Moll you're going to lodge me with?" he asked instead.

"She's m' sister." The fisherman's hand on his shoulder steered him down the muddy street. Edoran's boots were already ruined, so he made no protest. "Her husband was a rover—he took off for the towns, finally, and left her here. She's got no children of her own, but there's a hired boy, Mouse. He's a bit older than you," Togger added. "He can show you how to go on."

As if he needed a hired boy to teach him manners. But most of Edoran's attention was taken up by the house they were approaching. It was a little smaller than most of the huts, and made of the same weathered wood and thatch. It looked as if in the summer it had flower boxes below the windows, and maybe flowers in the muddy beds in front of the house as well, but now it was all drab and barren in the late-winter sun.

Togger rapped on the door. The woman's voice within hadn't even finished replying when he lifted the latch and led the reluctant prince inside.

It was dark, despite the fire crackling on the hearth and the sun that came through the thick glass circles that filled the windows.

Edoran looked around, paying little attention as Togger explained his presence to the fisherwife. The furniture was sturdy and graceless, though not as rough as he'd expected, with patchwork cushions on the seats. This was clearly the hut's main room, used for both sitting and casual dining, like the central room of Edoran's own suite in the palace. The other door probably led to the woman's bedchamber.

Edoran suddenly realized that Togger had fallen silent, and both of them were looking at him.

"Where do I sleep?" he asked. "And might I have a bath soon? It's been some days since I've been able to clean myself."

The woman was all faded—clothes, blue eyes, and her long, graying hair. She blinked in surprise, though Edoran couldn't understand why. Togger had just told her that he'd been on the run from the guard, so his unwashed state shouldn't astonish her.

"I can see why you'd want one," she said. "And you can sleep in the loft with Mouse. By the time you get back, I'll have found you some better clothes than that ragged stuff. I'll heat some water, and you can be clean in clean clothes for your dinner. How does that sound?"

That sounded wonderful, except . . . "Back? Where am I going?"

"Nowhere bad. Gart brought in a pakkie catch last night, so everyone's down at the gutting shed today, earning a share of the profit. I'll take you there next." Togger's hand fell on his shoulder once more. "When your pa sends for you, you'll be able to take him a bit of coin!"

He sounded as if this was a wonderful thing, and Edoran cast him an appalled glance. "You want me to gut fish? I don't know how!"

"That's all right." Togger's hand felt more like the grip of a jailer than the support Edoran thought he intended. "I'll teach you. It's not hard, once you've the knack of it."

He was already leading Edoran out of Moll's house and down toward the beach. The gutting shed wasn't something Edoran would have considered a shed, for it had no walls at all, only a thatch roof supported on poles. There was a long table beneath the roof, however, surrounded by fisherfolk with assorted barrels between them.

The barrels would hold the fish, Edoran guessed, either those the crowd had finished with or those still in possession of their guts. He had often eaten fish and enjoyed it. Preparing them to be eaten shouldn't be too hard. The smell wasn't as bad as he'd expected; the catch was clearly fresh, and the cold wind that blew off the sea, cutting through his britches and creeping up under his coat, also dispersed the stench.

The table, Edoran saw as they drew nearer, was covered with small, silvery fish. The men and women around the table—all of whom eyed him curiously, as Togger once more explained his presence—were to gut the fish and then pass them to someone who would sprinkle them with salt and pack them into one of the large barrels that mingled with the smaller ones. Simple. Edoran could do this.

He held to that thought, shyly returning some of the fisherfolk's smiles as he took his place in the line—he might have to stay here for some days, after all.

"Here's what you do," Togger told him. "Take a fish and get a good grip on it. No, you've got to hold it belly up, like this, for you open the belly to get at the guts."

Edoran corrected his grasp as Togger showed him. The fish was slippery, both stiff and limp at the same time, but he got a firm grip on it and took the small knife Togger handed him.

"This is how you do it." The fisherman took up another knife and a fish of his own. "You insert the tip of the knife, blade up, into this hole near the tail, then cut the skin all the way up to between its gills. Like this."

One smooth stroke laid open the dead fish's belly. That wasn't so bad. But then Togger thrust his thumbs into the incision and pushed out a mass of slimy, pulpy, bloody stuff. . . .

Edoran's stomach heaved. He turned hastily toward one of the small barrels and saw that its bottom was covered with fish guts. He barely made it to the water's edge before the contents of his stomach came up, splattering the sand.

He heard the fisherfolk's laughter over the roaring of the surf, and over the roar of blood in his ears.

"Don't feel badly, lad." Togger had come up behind him. "It

takes some that way at first. Indeed, some never take to gutting, which is why Moll's making up supper for half a dozen families, instead of working down here picking up a better wage."

"I made a mess of it," Edoran said bitterly. "I always make a mess of it."

"The gulls'll clean that right up," said Togger, misunderstanding. "And the tide'll take what's left."

Edoran's stomach churned again at the thought of gulls picking over his vomit, but he suppressed the nausea and stood. "I'd prefer to assist Mistress . . . ah, Goodwife Moll in her cooking."

"Aye, that's likely best. For today, at least," said Togger.

As far as Edoran was concerned, it would be forever before he returned to the gutting shed.

Mistress Moll took the news of his weakness calmly and set him to peeling potatoes, yet another task performed with a small, sharp knife. Though the job didn't trouble his stomach, Edoran's peelings were thick, clumsy chunks, not the long, thin strips the fisherwife produced.

Mouse, the hired boy, came in to get a bag of salt from the cellar stores. Instead of the mouselike boy Edoran had expected, he was a hulking youth of eighteen, taller than most men, his arms thick with muscle.

Goodwife Moll started to introduce them, but Mouse shrugged her off. "Togger told us about him, down at the shed." He glanced at the pile of peelings on the table in front of Edoran. "He says the sand man wants him to go out with the boats, but if he can't use a knife better than that . . ."

He shrugged again and departed, ignoring Edoran's glare.

"Don't pay him any mind, Ron," Moll told him. "He's a young lout. They mostly are, at that age. You're not doing badly, for a first try."

It took Edoran several seconds to remember who "Ron" was. "I was never taught this," he said.

"That's clear enough." Her pale eyes twinkled. "What are you trained for?"

Edoran opened his mouth, remembered he was supposed to be a merchant's son, and shut it again. "Ah, reading and writing out bills and invoices and things. And keeping account books."

He prayed that no one in the village would turn up with an account book and expect him to keep it. His father's journals had taught him to read, but there'd been nothing to teach him math.

"Hmm. Not much call for any of those things here," said Moll, to Edoran's great relief. "But we'll find plenty you can do, never fear."

That was what Edoran was afraid of.

The bath he'd been looking forward to turned out to be a basin of warm water and a cloth, with which he was expected to scrub himself all over. At least he could manage that without assistance, and he did feel cleaner when he climbed into the clothing Moll had borrowed from her neighbors.

The canvas britches had been worn to softness, and the shirt, though rougher than he was accustomed to, was clean. If the bulky sweater made him feel like a sheep, well, blending into the flock was his goal. It fell almost to his knees, and after he'd worn it for a few minutes, he felt warm for the first time that day.

The dinner he'd helped prepare was, of course, fish stew. Edoran suppressed a lingering memory of fish guts welling over Togger's thumbs and ate several bowls.

He was beginning to think he might survive Caerfalas after all when Moll told him, rather firmly, that washing the dinner dishes would be his job.

"My . . . But . . . Isn't there someone else who could do it?" Edoran asked.

"Oh, aye." Mouse snorted. "I'll go get the invisible servants, who live in a barrel out back. No, you witheless loon, there's no one to do it but you."

"No need to take that tone, Mouse," said Moll. "Ron's probably a bit tired—and no wonder!"

But she didn't offer to do the dishes for him.

"He's not tired," said Mouse. "His Highness here just doesn't like to get his hands dirty."

Edoran's heart jolted in sudden fear, but Moll and Togger showed no reaction. Mouse hadn't suddenly figured out who he really was; he was just trying to be insulting. And he'd succeeded.

"I'll wash the dishes," Edoran told them stiffly. With the training Arisa had given him at the inn, he managed to do it with only a few corrections from Moll, who had relented enough to dry for him.

Over the next few days Edoran discovered a host of chores he couldn't do—or, at best, did badly.

It turned out there was no one his own age among the villagers, though there were a handful of seventeen- and eighteen-year-olds and a mob of younger children.

The older ones, he soon learned, followed Mouse's lead. Edoran was scornfully referred to as "Your Highness" whenever he botched a task. He didn't care what Mouse thought of him, but the nickname still stung—he had thought he was getting better at dealing with common people.

At least the children didn't care what their older brothers and sisters thought; they accepted Edoran's company so well that he often found himself assigned to keep an eye on them when their mothers were busy with their own work.

At one point he was even set, under Moll's supervision, to watching the babes. But he found their complex needs unnerving, and changing diapers was even more disgusting than gutting fish.

Edoran preferred the ones who were old enough to take care of their own needs, but too young to regard him with the contempt of the teens—or the more distant reserve their parents displayed.

It was the children who showed him the old keep. There wasn't much left of it. Judging by the foundation, the tower that had once held some local chieftain and his family had never been large, even before it had collapsed in ruins. The outer walls had been built of blocks too large for the locals to tear down and reuse. A few stones had been dislodged by weather and time, but Edoran, walking the top of it all round the square, thought his father would have approved. It was both thicker and taller than the wall that surrounded the palace he now lived in.

It was also deserted, except when the children played there, and Edoran went to the fortress whenever he had free time. There he could shelter from the cold sea wind and relax in his own company, with no critical eyes upon him.

It seemed to him as if every time he drew a breath Moll found yet another dirty, demeaning task for him to muddle through. But he was glad that he was down on his hands and knees, scrubbing the floor of the meeting hall where the women had gathered to knit more sweaters, when the searchers arrived.

One of the teens, a plump girl with long hair braided down her back, slipped into the room to announce that there was an army patrol "looking for some young nobleman who's run away!"

Edoran froze, his hands wrapped in the filthy rag.

One of the women said, "Well, we've no nobles here," and several of them smiled.

He thought that Moll cast him a curious glance, but none of the others appeared to give his presence a thought, even when a pair of soldiers appeared in the doorway.

Edoran started to peek at them, then realized it would be less suspicious to stare openly. He didn't know much about army rank markings, but he thought the young officer was a lieutenant and the other a common soldier. They both looked equally bored.

"Fair morning, goodmen," said Moll politely. "I hear you're looking for a runaway."

"Yes, mistress." The lieutenant's accent proclaimed that he'd been born in the city—and not in its richer parts. It reminded

Edoran, achingly, of Weasel, and he returned to mopping the floor to hide his suddenly stinging eyes.

Sandeman had promised to find him, and everyone in the village said "Sandy" could be relied on.

The lieutenant went on to describe Edoran fairly accurately, though he never even glanced at the boy in the ragged britches and shaggy sweater.

Edoran wondered why they claimed to seek some anonymous young nobleman if the rumors of his disappearance were as widespread as Sandeman and Giles had claimed. Probably Holis and General Diccon were trying to keep that rumor from spreading out of the city.

Edoran scrubbed industriously at the floor. None of the adults in Caerfalas had ever called him "Your Highness," but it wouldn't do for them to start while the soldiers were there.

Fortunately, they soon left, and he could return to working at his usual pace—which involved spending as little time scrubbing as he could manage.

Even doing his best to avoid the worst chores, as the days progressed Edoran's hands roughened. He hated washing in cold water in the morning, and in only a basin at night. He hated work of all sorts. He would have hated sharing the loft with Mouse even if he hadn't snored.

He couldn't avoid Mouse during the day, either, for the hulking lout was forever showing him how to do this thing or that—none of them anything Edoran had the least desire to learn.

That morning, on his sixth day in Caerfalas, it was knots.

"Pay attention to this one, Your Highness," Mouse said. "Sandeman wants us to take you out with the boats, and if you muck this up it could cost us a net."

Edoran knew that there wasn't a man in the village who'd take him out on a boat. Not even Togger.

"You start with a loop, like this," Mouse went on. "Then you wrap the short end around it twice."

Edoran tried, the rope resisting his fingers like it was alive and wanted to thwart him. It hadn't escaped his notice that the fisherfolk despised him. But that was nothing new.

"Then you pull a fold of the long end through here to form another loop, and the short end goes through it. Then give it a yank." Mouse yanked, producing a tight, intricate knot with a loop at one end.

Edoran forced a bit of the long rope through the only loose place he could find, then tucked the short end through it and pulled . . . producing an ugly, intricate mess.

He sighed and let the rope fall to the floor. Maybe that would end the lesson, at least for—

Mouse's open palm cuffed the back of his head. The blow wasn't hard, but it was so unexpected that Edoran staggered.

"Pay attention!" Mouse snapped. "You're not even trying!"

Edoran stared at him, anger rising in his blood like steam from a kettle. He *had* been trying. He'd been shoving that rope around for what felt like hours, and this—this *lout* had dared to strike him! He could be flogged for that! Edoran could have the lot of them flogged, for the indignities they'd inflicted on him, for their lack of respect. If they'd known he was the prince . . .

His thoughts stopped. Time seemed to stop, as he stared at the idea, dazzled by its simplicity.

They didn't know he was the prince.

Not one person in this village, not even Togger and Moll, had any idea who he was. He'd always hated being Prince Edoran the incompetent, Prince Edoran the whiner . . . the prince that Pettibone had made.

He'd known that Pettibone had set out to make him look stupid, to keep him from learning anything worth knowing, to keep people, even the servants, from liking him. He still hadn't been able to avoid becoming that prince, even though he knew he was playing into his enemy's hands.

Now, for the first time, he had a chance to be someone else. He'd have to think about this some more, but right now he had a chance to be someone else . . . and he was failing.

He took a deep breath, picked up the rope, and turned to Mouse.

"Show me again." He tried to make it a request instead of a command, and he didn't think he succeeded, but Mouse showed him again. And again.

The fifth time through, Edoran's rope tightened into a loop. It wasn't as neat as the one Mouse made, but it was a knot instead of a muddle.

"Good, lad!" This time Mouse's hand clapped him on the shoulder. Edoran still staggered, but he didn't mind. A wide grin spread over his face.

He retreated to the old fortress to think, but the idea that had seized him only became clearer. He didn't know if he could be someone other than the Prince Edoran that Pettibone had created, but for the first time in his life he was facing people who knew nothing about him except what he showed them. He hadn't made much of a showing so far, but at least he could try.

He started really working at the tasks they set him. He hoped that trying to do them, instead of trying to avoid them, would make him good at what he did. Unfortunately, it didn't work out that way, but he did do better when he tried. And his effort was sufficiently visible that the adults praised him for it, offering tips that often made the task a bit easier . . . though the disgusting chores were still disgusting.

After a few days, even the teens stopped calling him "Your Highness." Now that he was working with them, Edoran noticed that they called one another worse names than that, and no one seemed to take offense.

During one of the women's sessions he asked Moll about her knitting, hoping that was something he might do. It would be more pleasant than carrying slops to the village pigpen.

"You throw the loop over the tip of this needle, then drag it under the other one, like so." She demonstrated slowly. Now that the needles had stopped flashing, Edoran saw that knitting consisted of tying a whole series of tiny knots. Using sticks instead of fingers. So much for him being able to knit. He sighed.

"That's a simple backstitch," Moll went on. "There are lots of other stitches, and shifting among them forms different patterns in the knitting. That's how we make our village pattern. We knit in family and name patterns too, so every sweater our lads wear out to sea tells folk they came from Caerfalas. And if a sweater comes back to us, we'll know whose it was."

"Whose it . . . You use those sweaters to identify the dead?"

"Not much left of a man's face, after he's been in the water for a week," Moll said matter-of-factly. "That's why the fishing villages first came up with different patterns. It's some comfort to know that your boy's finally come ashore, and been buried with care and respect, even if it was a stranger who did it. But it's not only that; our sweaters are our kin mark on friends and family. And we knit in luck symbols to draw the favor of the gods and keep our men from the sea."

"Favor of the God," said one of the women firmly, and several laughed.

"Or of the One God," Moll conceded. "If you don't want to spread your bets a bit."

"What's the use of calling for the attention of gods who don't care about man?" another woman asked, and a theological argument ensued.

Edoran had heard several such debates in the past few weeks. In Caerfalas, and perhaps in other fishing villages, some folk followed the One God and some the Hidden faith . . . and no one cared. No Hidden priests were turned over to the authorities for hanging, and if a child wandered off, people turned out and found it, instead of accusing their neighbors of stealing it for sacrifice.

This wouldn't have been possible in the city, or any large town, and as for the farming villages . . . Edoran didn't know enough about the inner life of the villages he'd passed through even to guess.

He looked at the pattern on the front of his sweater, recognizing it for the first time as the same one that decorated all the sweaters around him.

"Whose sweater am I wearing?" he asked Moll.

"Oh, we never give someone's sweater to anyone else. Especially at sea, but even on land that's asking for bad luck. You're wearing a stranger's sweater, with the Caerfalas pattern, but no family or personal name in it. But it does hold luck signs for Luric and Rish, and the narrow god as well."

"The One God," another woman corrected her.

Moll grinned. "We don't hand out many stranger's sweaters," she told Edoran. "If it should return to us empty . . . well, we'd know it was you we'd lost."

Edoran doubted he was about to be lost, but this sweater that held no family and no name . . . it felt as if he'd actually become no one. After a moment, he decided he liked that feeling.

He gave up on trying to knit. His favorite task was still tending the children, but now he was learning their names, and those of their parents, and he sometimes joined their games.

Many of them were spending more time with their fathers now, for the fishermen planned to set out to sea in less than a week. The children led Edoran down to where the beached boats were being scraped and rigged, and he saw that the luck signs he'd seen on the sweaters were also being painted onto their hulls.

Togger set him to mending nets, which was at least less

complex than knitting. Edoran learned that soon great schools of bluefish would be migrating through the straits. They always did so in the early spring, and the signs—though he never learned exactly what signs—indicated that they'd be earlier than usual this year.

The men told tales as they worked, mostly of comical mishaps, but also of storms that blew up unexpectedly and sent the ships racing to strange shores it took weeks to return from. They also spoke of the need for new tiller straps, or a new set of sails. Edoran slowly realized that the bluefish migration—whatever a bluefish was—was the longest and most profitable voyage the fishermen would make all year. His tentative hopes of being included dropped even lower. Judging by their tales, there was no place on this important voyage for a clumsy amateur.

But helping the rest of the village during their men's absence was important too, Moll informed him, and Edoran resigned himself to staying. So much so that when a peddler came through, selling pots and pans, ribbons and lace, he took notice of a bag of hard candy in the man's pack. With the men gone, Edoran would no longer be able to threaten his young charges with telling their fathers if they made trouble . . . but perhaps he could bribe them.

Moll had neatened up the ragged edge of his collarless shirt, exclaiming over the fine "city" linen, but she'd deemed his britches past mending. The peddler also sold buttons, and Edoran delved into Moll's rag bag and cut off the button that had fastened his waistband. It was made of polished bone, not silver or brass, but some craftsman had carved a stag's head onto its face, and the work was finer than anything in the peddler's button box.

The man was impressed by the workmanship, though he haggled long and hard. Eventually a bag of candy changed hands. And if three-quarters of it was gone before the fishermen left the village, well, those children's skill in argument could have put law clerks to shame. Edoran had never been taught the art of negotiation, so how could he resist?

He was more concerned about his diminishing supply of candy than anything else, and when Moll shook him awake one day before dawn, Edoran's first thought was that he'd left some chore undone.

"What?" he asked blearily. "Did I— Is it Sandeman? Has he come for me?" His heart leaped at the thought, and then, strangely, sank. And that was ridiculous, because he wanted to see Weasel again more than anything else. But why would Sandeman come for him in the middle of the night?

"It's not Sandy." Moll turned to wake Mouse as well. "It's the tide."

"The what?" Edoran knew what the tide was, he just couldn't think why it would necessitate rousing him at—he reached out with his sensing and found the position of the sun—more than two hours before dawn.

Mouse rubbed his face, yawning. "It's the tide, loon. We're launching the boats when it goes out, so if you want a hot meal on a table that holds still, you'd better get dressed—this will be your last for quite a while."

CHAPTER 8

THE ONE OF STONES

The One of Stones: abundance. A rich harvest.
Wealth. A good life.

8

They launched the boats as the first glimmer of dawn touched the water. The tide was near its height, so they didn't have to drag the hulls far over the sand.

Every man in the village grasped the ropes they strung around the first boat, their feet digging into the sand until the hull shifted and began to slide. They pulled the boat right into the cold surf, soaking boots, britches, and sweaters in the chest-deep water.

Edoran, shorter than the others, found himself floating in the deeper waves and had to swim back to shore. But he made himself useful there, running ropes around the next boat. If Togger was willing to take him to sea, he *would* be useful. He would make sure the fisherman never regretted it, not once.

After pulling each boat into the cove, the fishermen anchored it and swam back to shore, so all could help with the other boats. Edoran had thought it would take a long time to launch the whole fleet, almost two dozen of them, but the tide had only started to go out when they dragged the last boat out past the surf, and it began to rise off the sand with the pull of each wave, then to float in the surging water.

When the next wave picked Edoran up, Togger grabbed a double handful of his sweater and thrust him up the side of the hull till he could grab the railing. Edoran was still scrabbling his way aboard when Togger and several others climbed over the rail, but he managed to get himself onto the deck of Togger's boat before one of the others had to help him.

Most of the men were now swimming out to their own boats. Mouse was sailing with Togger, Edoran knew, and five other men, two of whom had lost their boat to a reef several years ago. The other three were boys not much older than Mouse who were hoping to earn enough to buy their own boats someday. Edoran had learned that from listening to their talk on the beach.

As they lowered the sails and the boat leaped through the waves, with the sun streaming down to dry his clothes, and the wind fresh off the sea, Edoran could think of no reason any man would desire anything else in life.

An hour later, he couldn't imagine why anyone would want to go near the sea. Ever. Miles away would be too close.

Mouse paused in doing something mysterious with a rope to clap him on the back. "Don't worry, runt. It takes a lot of folk that way at first. You want to die now, but come morning you'll be fine."

Edoran wondered if "runt" was better than "Your Highness." And he didn't want to die; he just wanted this accursed tub to stop bouncing so his head could stop spinning. . . . His stomach heaved once more.

"I hate you," he muttered when the paroxysm eased.

Mouse's grin held just enough sympathy to keep Edoran from trying to punch him. That, and the fact that Mouse was twice his size, and the deck was swaying up and down, and his stomach . . . Edoran returned hastily to the rail.

When his stomach finally realized there was nothing more to come up, and hadn't been for some time, it was Mouse who dragged him away from the rail and laid him down on a bedroll in the bow of the ship, where Edoran could lie in the fresh air and still keep out of the others' way. It was one of the other men who brought him a cup of hot mint tea and insisted he try, at least, to drink it. To Edoran's astonishment, after the first precarious sips it settled his stomach, and the mint cleared the foul taste from his mouth. He barely woke when they carried him below and tucked him into his berth.

In the morning he discovered that Mouse had been right—the boat still bobbed like a cork in a millrace, but the air was clear, the sea sparkled, and Edoran was actually hungry! He threw out his arms and spun in sheer delight at being there, out on a boat with the men, and not even sick anymore.

"That's better now, isn't it?" Togger asked, coming up behind him.

Edoran grinned. "What should I do?"

In those first days there was little he could do, for the boats were only casting around the straits in search of their quarry. Edoran tried to master the complicated web of rope that controlled the sails, but his knots still had a tendency to come undone, and no one trusted him to do more than pull on one rope or gradually release another.

On their fourth day at sea, the man who perched on the mast

of a neighboring ship began shouting and waving his arms. Edoran, down on the deck, was too busy obeying the sudden spate of snapped commands to look for what the scouts were seeing. The big booms that held the nets were loosed from their rests, and the nets were rigged to fall.

Then Togger shouted and the men swung the booms out over the waves, the nets sinking slowly out of sight.

Peering over the railing, Edoran couldn't see anything, but as the sails pulled the boat forward he could feel the drag of the nets growing stronger and stronger. He didn't know how Togger knew they were full, but finally the fisherman called, "Enough! We've a load, lads, so pull 'em in."

The nets had been relatively light when they were lowered. Pulling them up took every man in the crew hauling on the draw lines. When the first net cleared the water, Edoran gasped. He'd expected a moderate load of smaller fish, but this net bulged with sleek, struggling, blue-green shapes. The smallest was as long as his forearm. The largest, he later learned, was longer than his whole arm, from shoulder to fingertips, but all he saw then was a mass of writhing fish and the flash of scales.

They swung the boom in and dropped their catch on the deck. The second net, whose sunken weight was now pulling the boat in a lazy circle, was dragged up to its boom and swung aboard by men who had to kick the flopping fish out of their way. They coshed the bluefish on the head to kill them as soon as they had time to do so, for Togger said the Lady frowned on hunters who let their prey suffer unnecessarily.

Mindful of his stomach, which was still sometimes queasy, Edoran left the gutting to the rest of the crew. But he was able to pack the cleaned fish in salt, and after the full barrels had been stowed in the hold, he helped wash down the deck with fresh seawater.

Edoran thought nothing of it when they cast the fish guts over the side, and he was startled when a fish almost as big as he was leaped out of the water right next to the railing.

"He's thanking us for the meal," Mouse said.

"They . . . they eat fish guts?" It sounded cannibalistic to Edoran.

"They eat fish," Mouse replied. "Guts and all. They're not fish themselves, though they live in the sea. They're warm-blooded, like we are, and sometimes they save men who've been knocked overboard and carry them to land. It's good luck to feed them."

"That's just a tale," one of the other men scoffed.

"No, it's not," another proclaimed. "They're cousins to man, and that's why they save us."

"Have you ever met anyone a dolphin saved?"

The debate went on, but Edoran, hanging over the side to watch, paid it no heed. Mouse came to stand beside him. "They're beautiful, aren't they?"

"They're incredible," Edoran said. "I've never seen anything like it. Look, another one's jumping!"

"They'll do that on and off for hours," Mouse informed him. "Crazy Cozzen can say what he likes, but I still think they're thanking us. You did a good job today, runt."

Runt again. Edoran turned to confront the older boy, but Mouse's eyes were on the waves, looking for dolphins. He hadn't even thought about calling Edoran runt, the prince realized. He called almost everyone by some nickname. It meant nothing. . . . It was doing a good job that mattered.

"Thanks," said Edoran calmly.

The small fleet sailed on in search of another school, and Edoran finally began to produce knots that would hold reliably. Now if he only understood the rigging . . .

The straits weren't as empty as Edoran would have thought. In addition to dolphins, who checked in with the boats from time to time, they encountered fleets from other villages bent on the same hunt. When that happened, one fleet or the other would alter their course and sail alongside as news was shouted back and forth.

The first thing to be discovered was the location of the last bluefish school they'd found, but there was also news of some kinsman or kinswoman who'd married into the other village and birthed a daughter, or sold a bit of carving for a good price, or built another room onto their house.

They passed islands, too small for people to live there, but with beaches where ships could put in to get fresh water and scrape their hulls. They passed other ships as well, merchant freighters or naval vessels, and dozens of others. Edoran couldn't tell, from a single glance at the sails and hull, what a ship's purpose was, but most of the men around him could. He also slowly realized that when they saw any ship that wasn't part of a fishing fleet, Togger wrote it down and noted the date and location.

One day a naval ship hailed them. After learning they were from Caerfalas, they sent a small boat to pick up Togger, who took his list of ships along with him.

He returned without it, several hours later, looking thoughtful and somber.

"What was that about?" Edoran asked.

Togger frowned at him, then sighed. "Sandeman brought you to us himself, so there's no harm in it," he said obscurely. "But I wouldn't tell this to just anyone, lad, and you'll keep it to yourself. Sandeman's trying to organize the fishing fleets to report all the boats they see to some friends of his in the navy, hoping they can finally lay hands on those accursed pirates."

"The pirates? But you don't know anything . . ." Edoran thought about it. "You do see their ships sometimes, don't you?"

"Aye, we do," Togger said grimly. "They leave us alone, for we've nothing worth stealing and pose no threat to them. A lot of the villages want to keep it that way. They say that if we start reporting pirate ships to the navy, they'll start sinking us. That our only defense is to not be worth the cost of powder and ball to send us to the bottom. But Sandeman says we've a duty to stop the murdering scum, and I agree. I don't think he's gotten any of the other villages to go along, but if the pirates keep raiding the coastal towns . . . We've not much worth stealing, but sooner or later they'll want something we have—clean water and fresh food, if nothing else. And then . . ."

Edoran remembered how that first raid had felt to his sensing. He shuddered.

"Are you sure it's safe to talk to the navy?" he asked. "I heard . . . In the city, I heard a rumor that someone in the navy was telling the pirates about naval ship movements. That's why the navy can't locate them, and why several naval ships have vanished. They say the pirates would have to know where they were searching to avoid them so consistently. Or to set up such an overwhelming ambush."

A frown creased Togger's brow. "The only captains who know to signal us are working with Sandeman. But if there's a traitor . . . Ron, how sure of this are you?"

Edoran remembered an argument he'd overheard between Holis and the Falcon—Holis claiming that the pirates had to be getting inside information, and the Falcon saying she couldn't believe any naval officer would ever work with the pirates.

The Falcon, who had then turned traitor and tried to kidnap the prince.

"Pretty sure. Sort of sure."

Togger sighed. "People who live by the sea, we know life's a chancy thing. What first seems good can be bad, and what seems bad can come to good in the end. That's the nature of water, and of life. But I must say, lad, I wish you were sure."

Edoran spent the rest of the day thinking about the Falcon taking Weasel away by sea. Arisa had been certain of that, and the Falcon had allies in the navy. If her daughter was right, if she had escaped by sea, was there a reason for it? Could her base, could Weasel himself, be hidden somewhere in the islands?

It was pure speculation, but it would explain why no one had found her on land, and it felt . . . right, in that part of his instincts he'd learned to trust.

Edoran resolved to examine any island they passed, and to ask the fleets they traded news with if they'd seen anything odd.

Edoran might not have been able to rig sails, but his days became busier as he learned to help the cook and perform dozens of other tasks essential to the smooth running of the ship. They found another school of bluefish, and while Edoran took care not to look at the fish guts, he could pitch them over the side after the crates were stowed, and watch the dolphins streak through the water to snatch them.

His arms and shoulders ached with the strain of hauling up the heavy nets and lowering full barrels into the hold, but it was a good ache, the ache of work well done. He was happy.

Ron the fisherboy was happy all the time, even when he was cold and wet and tired. Happy in a way that pampered Prince Edoran had never been in his life.

And the realm was running just fine without him.

Regent Pettibone had told him straight out that he didn't really need Edoran to rule Deorthas. *As long as you're more use to me alive, you'll stay alive,* he'd said after the prince had tried to run away. *Had* run away, and managed to elude the guard for more than two weeks before they found him and brought him back. *But if you become more trouble than you're worth . . .* He hadn't had to finish the threat. He hadn't been lying, either. The man who'd killed a king with no one the wiser could easily dispose of an inconvenient prince.

Edoran had never dared to run away again, never dared to defy his regent over any major matter, lest he make so much trouble that he'd no longer be "useful."

But he had to admit that Pettibone had run the realm as well as most of the kings of Deorthas—better than some of them. And if Pettibone hadn't been a bad ruler, surely Holis, or even the Falcon, could manage as well. He could give her the sword and shield and his promise to vanish forever if she'd let Weasel go. He'd be just another fisherman, caring more about the next catch than the conflicts among shareholders, townsmen, and country folk, caring nothing for the disputes between the university men and the One God's church.

The Falcon might even believe him. It would be true.

Of course, if Holis and the Falcon went to war over the throne, Weasel and Arisa would be horribly torn. Edoran sighed. He'd have to stop that, if he could. But Holis and the Falcon were really at war right now, and he couldn't see any way to stop them, prince or not. So maybe . . .

The prospect of changing his life permanently haunted him throughout the next few days.

Edoran kept a close watch on the islands they sailed among, and as they worked their way farther down the coast, there were a lot of them. The fisherfolk had described the islands in the eastern strait as a maze, and Edoran was beginning to understand why.

But he kept his eyes open, and it was in the middle of dealing with another bluefish catch that he glimpsed a flash of red. Not on an island, for there were no islands in sight, but on a ragged jut of rock, too small for fresh water or for the sturdiest scrub to grow. Edoran wasn't sure the top would be above the level of the waves in the higher tides, but the moon was half full now and the tides were low.

Low enough that something had washed onto the rocks and not blown off again?

The rocky outcrop was too small to hold a rebel camp or a prisoner, but the bit of color troubled Edoran enough that when the catch had been stowed below, he mentioned it to Togger.

"It's likely a bit of wreckage cast up there," the fisherman said. "The sea does that sort of thing. Pay it no heed."

But something was pricking at the part of Edoran's mind where his sensings made themselves felt. Not a warning, no great catastrophe. Not even a change in the weather, which had been amazingly fair. It was just . . .

"I think we should check it out," he told Togger. "There's something very odd about it."

Togger rubbed his bristling chin thoughtfully. None of the men had shaved in the past few weeks. "It's usually wise to check out odd things when you're at sea. And it's not as if we've a schedule to keep."

Turning the whole fleet and tacking back against the wind was so troublesome and time-consuming that Edoran regretted having said anything long before they neared the rock. Suppose it turned out to be nothing—which was likely! If Edoran should see something else on one of the islands, he'd never be able to persuade them to investigate. He might have jeopardized his chance to save Weasel, just because some scrap had washed up on the rocks at an odd angle.

They lowered sails as they drew nearer, having no desire to crash into the rocks themselves. Edoran was looking with the others as they approached, but it was the scout stationed on the mast who suddenly shouted, "There's a man on that rock! I think . . . Yes, it is a man! But he's not moving."

Dead or not, a castaway had to be retrieved. Togger's boat had no skiff, but one of the others did. As its crew rowed out to retrieve the man, or the body, as the case might be, the other boats maneuvered closer, till they were able to rope themselves together with bundles of net as bumpers between them. Everyone wanted to see if the dead man . . .

But he wasn't dead. A shout rang out from the rocks, and a moment later Edoran saw the crew helping someone climb down. He appeared to need a lot of help, but he was moving on his own. One of the crew picked up the scrap of red that had attracted Edoran's attention, and Edoran saw it was a woolen undershirt, the kind that navy sailors were issued.

As the skiff drew nearer, Edoran thought that the rest of the man's clothes looked like those of a navy sailor, but they were so tattered it was hard to be sure. The stranger was lying in the bottom of the skiff, and one of the fishermen helped him sip from a water flask.

They had to lift him over the side of Togger's boat, for his strength was gone. His skin was red with sunburn, his lips so cracked with thirst that they had bled.

He was trying to talk as they lifted him aboard, but Togger told him to be still and sent for a bedroll, blankets, and salve. Only when the man was settled, sipping more water while the cook heated broth, did Togger let him speak.

"Your ship was lost, I take it?" His voice was very gentle.

"Lost?" The man's voice was a husky rasp. "It wasn't lost. It was blown right out of the water by those pirate scum, curse them." Tears rose in his eyes, and several fishermen gasped.

"You look like navy to me," said Togger. "I've heard that naval ships in search of the pirates have been disappearing. But they're all armed, and better than the pirates are. How are they taking you down, without one naval victory in all those fights?"

He was planning to report the answer to Sandeman, Edoran realized, but the sailor began to laugh. Wild, bitter laughter, with sobs beneath.

Togger gripped his shoulder. "Steady, man. I'm sorry to be—"

"No," the sailor gasped. "Don't be sorry. You've saved my life, and I only pray you don't regret it. The pirates murdered every one of the *Protector's* survivors because they knew the answer to your question. Tried to kill me, too. I guess. I don't . . ." His voice began to shake again.

"Say it, lad," Togger told him. "If it's something pirates will kill to silence, they'd never believe you hadn't told us. So we might as well know."

"The navy ships." The man swallowed hard and took another sip from the flask. "The ones that vanished. That no one could figure how the pirates took 'em so easy . . ."

"Aye?" Togger demanded.

"They weren't sunk," the sailor said. "And they didn't vanish, either. They've all joined up with the pirates!"

CHAPTER 9

THE SIX OF STONES

The Six of Stones: compassion.
The desire to come to another's aid.

Several men cried out in astonished horror, and Togger's mouth tightened. "I'd like to let you rest, lad, but you're going to have to tell us why you think those naval ships . . . Gone over to the *pirates*? That can't be right!"

"Why I think that? Why I *think* that?" the sailor rasped. "It was the *Gauntlet* that sank us! We'd heard they disappeared," he went on. "That the pirates had sunk 'em. That's what we assumed about all the ships that have gone missing. Though that's what they'll think about the *Protector*, too," he added grimly. "And in our case, it'll be true. I wonder . . ." His voice trailed off.

"You can't leave the story there," Togger told him.

"What? Oh. Well, when we saw the *Gauntlet*, we were thrilled. I mean, we'd given them up for lost. We sailed alongside, and the captain hailed her. He was talking to the *Gauntlet*'s captain, shouting back and forth, trying to find out what had happened to her. I see now that their captain was stalling," the sailor went on. "But at the time . . . It made sense he'd be asking for news, for orders, since he'd been out of touch so long. Even when they ran out their guns, we thought they were just drilling or some such thing. Our gun ports weren't even open when they fired." His voice was full of anger and pain. "We never had a chance. A shot from the second volley hit our powder and blew the *Protector* to splinters."

The crew was stunned into silence by this, but he went on without prompting. "I think the captain and officers died when the magazine went—they were mostly on the aft deck. There were only about a dozen of us, and most were wounded, when their small boats pulled us out of the water and they took us aboard."

"But . . . I mean . . . How can you be sure the pirates hadn't captured the ship, killed all her crew, and set her sailing under their own colors?" Togger asked.

"Our captain knew their captain personally," the man said. "And I recognized several of the *Gauntlet's* crew when we were taken aboard. Free, and serving with the pirates of their own will, the One God rot their bones."

The anger in his voice left no room for doubt.

"Why did they pick you up?" Edoran asked him.

"They said they wanted information. What our orders were, where we'd planned to search. But I think they were mostly making sure there were no survivors. None of us knew anything about our orders. How could we? That's officers' business. The first few they questioned told them that, and they coshed them unconscious and dropped them over the side. The next few tried to lie—claimed they'd heard officers talking, or that the bosun had told 'em our course. But the pirates broke their heads and pitched them over too. I don't know what I said. I tried to fight, I do remember that. Maybe that's why they missed their stroke."

"Missed?" Togger asked.

"They must have," the man said. "I don't remember being coshed, or going over the side, but I came round a bit when I hit the water.

Enough to know that if I splashed and made a fuss they'd launch a boat and make sure of me. My head felt like someone had driven a spike into it, but I turned my face to the side just enough to breathe and floated. The boat was drifting away by then. I think I was one of the last they dumped. But not the last, because I remember at least one splash, and then their mate's voice yelling to get the sails up. That they had just a week to make it to Boralee and burn it."

Several men exclaimed in shocked dismay.

"Boralee?" Edoran asked.

"A port town, not too far down the coast from here," said Togger. "You're sure you heard that?" he asked the sailor.

"'Get those sails up, you lazy wharf rats,'" the sailor quoted. "'We've just a week to reach Boralee and burn it.' I heard him clear as I hear you now, and it's not a thing a man forgets. But there was nothing I could do about it, adrift as I was. Once they were gone, I swam back to where the Protector sank and found a bit of deck that was big enough to float. The sea carried me down the coast, but there was never a glimpse of land. The wood was getting waterlogged, floating almost three inches under the surface, when I saw those rocks, and if the tide hadn't pulled me ashore in all that time it wasn't likely to, so I swam over there. I hoped there'd be fresh water...."

He licked his lips and took another drink.

"How long ago was that?" Togger asked urgently. "How long ago did the Protector sink?"

The sailor frowned. "I—I don't really know. I was on the wreckage at least two days . . . maybe. After I crawled up on the rocks I slept some. I think . . . I think three days, but I'm not sure."

"That's good enough." Togger patted his shoulder. "You've done your part, my friend. Rest now."

"How far are we from Boralee?" Edoran asked, although the crew's grim faces told him the answer wouldn't be good.

"At least five days' sail," said Togger. "Unless we cut through the islands, in which case . . . The wind is with us, but if he drifted with the current, it's with the pirates, too. Assuming that doesn't change . . ."

"It won't," Edoran told him. "Not for at least a week."

Togger cast him a curious glance, but he went on, "We know the islands well enough to sail between them, even at night, so we might be able to cut a day off of that. But it's still four days' sailing at the best speed we can manage."

"That might be enough!" Edoran exclaimed. "And if he's only been adrift two days . . ."

Togger rubbed his chin. "By the look of him, I'd say three days, maybe four. But who knows what might have delayed the *Gauntlet*? We've got to try to warn that town if there's any chance at all. Even if we're too late to help them, we can get this man to the guard to tell his story. That naval ships may have gone over to the pirates is something the regent has to know as soon as possible. So cast off those moorings, friends. We're sailing!"

They sailed both day and night for the next three days, sleeping in shifts. Remembering the dark rocks the sailor had been marooned on, Edoran finally asked Togger, "Is it safe this close to shore with so little moonlight?"

"No," said Togger. "Not unless you know the hazards of these waters as well as a landsman knows the path to his own privy."

He sounded confident, but Edoran had to ask, "Do you know these waters that well?"

Togger was silent long enough to make him nervous. "In parts," he said finally. "And the other men know other parts, so among us we'll be able to avoid the rocks and reefs. There's always some risk, sailing in the darkness. But even if it costs us a ship or two, we have to try. If we can warn those townsfolk in time for them to evacuate—or better yet, get a dozen guard troops there—it would be worth it."

Edoran now understood how much ships cost, and how hard they were to replace.

"Why did the pirates have to be there in a week? Why would it matter to them if Boralee burned eight days from now, or twelve?"

"I've been wondering about that myself," said Togger. "I've a couple of thoughts. The first is that it'll take more than the crew of one ship to sack a town that size. They're probably rendez-vousing with several other ships, maybe their whole fleet. And while that's bad in one way, because it increases our chances of coming across 'em, it's good in another, because some of those other ships might be delayed. My second thought is that they have some information about where the army patrols are, and that's the date when the largest number of troops are farthest from Boralee. Which is nothing but bad, any way you look at it."

"Are we going to be in time?" Edoran asked quietly.

Togger sighed. "I honestly don't know. We have to try. And we've made good time. We'll be there late tomorrow. The best a man can do is the best he can do."

It wasn't good enough. All the fishermen watched, throughout that next day's sailing, but it was the scouts who first saw the smoke. Soon Edoran could see it himself, a great dirty column, rising against the light of the lowering sun.

He'd been willing the ships to hurry for four days, as they raced before the wind. Now dread made the pace that had seemed so slow feel much too fast.

At least the pirates had gone. There were no sails in sight as they scudded up the coast and turned into Boralee's harbor.

The ships that had been moored at the dock were still burning, their masts charred skeletons in the cloudless sky.

The fishermen sailed their boats past the docks, right up the beach, till the sand grated under their hulls. Then they leaped out and ran. Edoran knew the tide was going out, so the boats would be safe. No excuse . . . no need for him to stay there.

At least it wasn't work he was trying to avoid. He could already feel it, in the part of his mind where his sensing lived, a red-hot anguish of loss and rage and grief.

He climbed over the railing and splashed through the surf, following the fishermen toward the burning town. As he saw when he reached the first major street, however, not all the town was burning. Only a few buildings were ablaze, though more were beginning to burn. The smoke stung his eyes.

The townsfolk were trying to put out the fires that hadn't taken hold yet, organizing bucket lines. Others went from one ragged pile of clothing to the next, seeing if any of the fallen still lived, or perhaps searching for missing friends and family. Edoran already knew that most of them were dead, a sensing that tasted of steel and ashes on the back of his tongue.

How best could he help?

He was about to join a bucket line when the girl caught his eyes. She sat with her back to him, not fallen, but sitting still in the midst of smoke and chaos. She wore a boy's coat and britches, and Edoran would have taken her for a boy except for the long dark hair that tumbled down her back.

She might be hurt, or maybe worse, and the thought of dealing with so much pain made Edoran cringe. But if she continued to sit there, someone would run her down, and if he couldn't help her, maybe he could get her to someone who could.

He'd almost reached her when a nearby wall collapsed in a burst of flame, and the long hair glinted with copper and maroon lights.

Arisa.

He ran the last few steps and fell to his knees beside her. He couldn't see any blood, but her face was pale and oddly blank.

"Are you hurt?" he asked urgently. "What's wrong?"

She didn't look at him. Edoran wasn't sure she recognized him, but she drew a shaking breath and spoke. "I couldn't reach her. She used to pay attention to me. To listen, sometimes. But she's in some other place now, and no matter what I say it doesn't get through."

The expression in her eyes, fixed on the burning buildings, sent a chill down Edoran's spine. He had to get her out of this, but where . . . ?

"Come with me." He put all the command he could into his voice, and it seemed to work. At least she allowed him to help her to her feet, and walked where he led her through the seething crowd down to the beach, where the air was fresh off the sea and the crash of the waves overwhelmed the distant shouts.

He found several blankets lying on the trampled sand—had the pirates bundled loot into them, to carry down to the shore? He folded one and seated Arisa on half of it, then wrapped another clumsily around her. Sitting down beside her reminded him of a folded rug, not so long ago.

"Remember when we were locked in that closet?" he asked.

She said nothing. Her gaze was on the waves, but Edoran didn't think she was seeing them. He reached out and touched her chin, turning her face toward him. "Remember when we were locked in that closet?"

She blinked, and then frowned. "Of course. What are you doing here?"

Relief washed through Edoran at the familiar, critical tone. "I'll tell you when you've told me."

Her gaze shifted aside. She pulled away from his hand and looked at the waves.

"I mentioned the closet," said Edoran, "because of the way you tried to beat down that door. I thought you were going to break an arm or something, before you'd quit."

She had thrown herself at it like a madwoman, though it was obvious from the start that she couldn't break it.

"So?" Her voice was harsh with suppressed tears.

"It's just . . . There's no door here. All you have to do is stop beating yourself against whatever it is, and tell me."

Two tears rolled down her face. She brushed them aside. "You're right. The thing is . . . I found my mother."

He'd already figured that one out. Her mother was the only person who could put her into this state. Maybe if she worked up to it gradually, the telling would be easier.

"How did you find her?"

"She left a message at one of the drops, just like I thought she would." Her breathing was easier now, and she went on without prompting. "That was two days after Giles took off with you. I wanted to follow you, but I thought—"

"Weasel was in more danger," Edoran cut in. "I thought so too. And I got rescued anyway, so go on."

Her glance was mildly curious, but she had too much on her mind to question him, and he was glad. He was tired of being rescued and had no desire to discuss his escape.

"She was expecting me to bring Holis' response to her demands," said Arisa. "I caught up with her just a few days after we parted, and I told her she'd got Weasel instead of you. She'd sent him by sea, but she rode with the men who went out the gates to draw the pursuit, because she knew that was the more dangerous job. She's not a coward!"

She glared at Edoran, daring him to deny it, but he'd never questioned the Falcon's courage. It was her sanity he doubted.

"Is Weasel all right?" That was what he cared about most.

"Of course. She wouldn't let me see him, but she knows Holis loves him. Any hostage is better than a . . . than none. I think she's got him hidden on another of the islands."

Another of the islands. "So her base is on an island? I had a feeling it might be."

"You and your feelings." Her shoulders slumped. "You're right, of course. She took me there when she realized that she had to make new plans."

"Was she angry with you?" Edoran asked. "I mean, you were the one who kept her from kidnapping me."

The girl's gaze fell. "I didn't tell her. She assumed that it was Weasel who figured it out. I'd just turned up, lugging the shield and sword along. She assumed . . ." Her voice was so soft now that Edoran could barely hear her. "She just assumed I was on her side. Like always."

The tears were falling again.

"She doesn't intend to kill you," Arisa went on fiercely. "Not you, or Weasel, or even Holis, unless she has to. She's going to claim that you gave her the shield and sword and asked her to be your regent. That you said you think Holis is incompetent. That he can't even keep the realm safe . . . safe from the pirates."

"Well, how could he?" Edoran asked. "They've got some spy in the navy who's telling them where the naval ships are looking for them."

He'd hoped to surprise, maybe even impress her with this, but she just nodded.

"She's not evil," Arisa said. "She isn't!"

"I never said she was." Thinking it was another matter.

"She plans to bring Holis down by creating dissent over the way he's handling the raids," Arisa went on. "She's already started rumors about how badly he's managing it. Then, when she's in control of the government and the raids stop, that will give her the support she needs to keep anyone from challenging her claim to the regency. When you turn twenty-two, she'll just let you be king in name while she goes on running things."

It was more likely she would kill him, whatever she'd told Arisa, but Edoran didn't care about that anymore. "How could she possibly stop—"

"She won't kill you!" Arisa insisted. "She says she'd never need to, that Pettibone ruined you, and you'd be perfectly happy to let someone else take over all the difficult ruling things while you live in luxury."

"I probably would," said Edoran. "But how can she stop the pirate raids when Holis couldn't? Even if she gets rid of their spies in the navy, they . . ."

Then it hit him. Why Arisa looked so miserable. Why the Falcon's main bases were all on islands. Even why the pirates had started raiding ashore, for the first time in anyone's memory.

"She's behind them?" His voice scaled up incredulously, but it wasn't really a question. "She's been behind them from the start! Of course she has. Her allies were always in the navy, and those are the ships that vanished! No wonder the pirates always knew who was hunting for them, and where and when, even on land—the Falcon was in charge of the hunt! How can you claim she's not evil? They've killed dozens of people! Maybe hundreds! And destroyed I don't know how much property, and wounded others who didn't die, and—"

"I know!" Arisa interrupted bitterly. "I know all of that . . . now. It took me a while to figure it out. To realize that all those rough men around the camp weren't just common sailors she'd recruited to the cause. They didn't talk much in front of me, but after a while little things started adding up. And I had to be sure, so I started spying on them deliberately."

She would have to be sure. The Falcon's daughter had inherited all her mother's courage, and then some. If it had been his mother, and he'd been trapped on an island surrounded by pirates, Edoran thought he'd have taken great pains not to learn the truth.

"I might have been able to live with that," Arisa said. "This is a war, even if there aren't armies marching around the countryside, and people die in wars. Even innocent people, sometimes. And she wasn't responsible for those deaths! She told the raiders to avoid killing anyone if they could. But . . . they're pirates. It got out of hand. That's why she started sending the navy ships with them, to keep the deaths to a minimum. So I think—I think I could have lived with that. Except . . . I heard . . . I was spying on all their meetings by then."

If she'd gotten through this much without faltering, what was the trouble now? Edoran suppressed a chill of dread. "Go on."

She took a deep breath and turned to face him. "There's a village of fishermen who've been reporting on pirate-ship movements to the navy. Holis' navy. The honest one."

Horror stopped Edoran's heart.

"Evidently, word of that's spreading up and down the coast," Arisa went on. "Some other villages are thinking about reporting them too. The pirates told my mother that if that happens, soon the navy will know exactly where they are. They said the fishermen are everywhere and see everything. So the pirates wanted to burn that village to the ground and kill everyone in it. As a warning to the others. Stop the rot before it has a chance to grow, they said. And . . ." She took another breath and went on, in a firm, clear voice that was the bravest thing Edoran had ever heard. "And my mother agreed."

"When? When is this raid going to take place?"

"I don't know, exactly. This attack is just a diversion. They're staging another, up the coast, so troops will be drawn away from the village from both directions. So there's no chance for anyone to reach it in time." Her voice was still clear, but the tears were falling once more. "They'll sail up the coast, meet up with the other half of the fleet, and then go in. I don't know exactly when, but it'll be soon, and if we're going to warn this Caerfalas in time . . ."

"We will." Edoran drew a shuddering breath, trying to calm his own galloping panic. "If the pirates just left here . . . They'll have to sail around the islands, and that will cost them some time. Then they'll have to rendezvous with the other ships and make their plans. We can beat them there. Evacuate. We'll save Caerfalas. You don't have to cry."

"It's not the cursed village," Arisa snapped. "Though I'm glad to see those ships. Don't you understand? My mother agreed to this! She agreed to let them kill all those people, just for trying to stop the pirates, who *she* turned loose in the first place. She—she's gone."

She was sobbing now, bitter, wrenching sobs that Edoran had no idea how to deal with. What would Ron the fisherboy do? *Try.*

He moved closer and put his arm around her shaking shoulders, just holding on, and eventually her weeping quieted.

"When I heard them talking about killing all those people, I knew I had to escape," said Arisa wearily. "To warn them. To . . . to do something. If Mother's men succeed in this, there won't be enough left of her to save. So I stowed away on the first ship to leave for the raid—"

"You stowed away on a *pirate* ship?" Edoran asked. She was the craziest girl.

"How else could I get there to warn anyone? Besides, I'm their leader's daughter. Even if they caught me, they couldn't do much. But they wouldn't have let me go ashore, so I had to be careful. I planned to go over the side first chance I got, find the nearest guard troop, and tell them . . . well, everything. But the first chance I had to go ashore was here, and it took awhile to tie the sword and shield to an empty keg, so they wouldn't sink, and I had to swim—"

"You've still got the sword and shield?" asked Edoran incredulously. "Here? With you?"

"They're hidden in a bush where I came ashore," said Arisa. "The current pulled me down the coast a ways. I couldn't leave them in my mother's hands. They're the only things that might make her listen to me now."

Her eyes were dry, but her voice was full of despair. And she wasn't the despairing type. Edoran regarded her with concern.

"I'll listen to you," he told her, relinquishing his pride. "And so will the men of Caerfalas—whether you've got the sword and shield or not. But I'm going to need your help, so don't you go and crumple up on me!"

She snorted at that. "All right, Your Highness. What do you intend to do now?"

CHAPTER 10

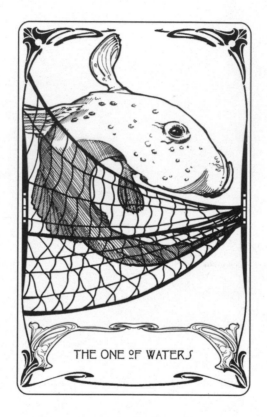

THE ONE OF WATERS

The One of Waters: the fish. An opportunity,
which may or may not be taken.

10

"I have . . . I think I have a plan." And in that plan Edoran saw an opportunity that took his breath away. "I have to think it through," he went on, "and check some things. Time is the most important. And the men of Caerfalas might not go along with it. The most important thing of all is to keep the village safe."

"Of course." There was only defeat in her voice. Even if his plans came off, the best her mother could expect was to be banished in disgrace.

But a part of his heart quivered with hope. In all the chaos that would ensue— or could be made to seem like it had ensued — surely there would be a chance for Prince Edoran to die. And if he died, then Ron the fisherboy would be free to live.

"Come on, then." Edoran pulled Arisa to her feet. "First we have to talk to Togger."

Arisa was startled to learn that men on the boats on the beach, those who'd come to the town's assistance, were from Caerfalas themselves. But the pirate raids were staged to draw troops away from Caerfalas, and because fishing fleets tried not to stray too far from their base, it made sense that they'd be somewhere in the vicinity. If they'd sailed down the coast in the other direction, they might have seen the smoke from the other diversionary raid and gone to investigate it.

But she was astonished when Edoran asked her not to reveal his true identity. "Aren't they more likely to listen to their prince than a common . . . whatever you're pretending to be?"

"If you knew nothing about me except the reputation Pettibone spread, would you listen to anything Prince Edoran suggested?"

Arisa eyed him. "I know you much better than that. *That's* why I wouldn't listen. What is this plan of yours, anyway?"

There was a time when Edoran would have been hurt by her teasing, but Mouse had cured him. He grinned. "Just for that, I'm not saying. No, seriously, I'll have to tell all of them, so I might as well do it once."

They found Togger helping the Boralee townsfolk dig a trench grave for the pirates who'd been killed during the raid. The dead townsfolk, of whom there were far more, were being washed and shrouded by their families.

Arisa watched bodies tumble into the trench, dumped willy-nilly. Her face was expressionless, but so pale that her freckles stood out like stars. Was she thinking of her mother being buried in a criminal's grave like this? Thinking that she *deserved* to be?

Edoran realized that he would have to try to save the Falcon, too, and grimaced.

He pulled Togger away from the others when they took up their shovels, and swiftly told him who Arisa was and how she'd come to Boralee. Togger was frankly incredulous of Arisa's claim to be the Falcon's daughter, but news of the threat to Caerfalas wiped all the doubt and humor from his expression.

"Can we beat them back to the village?" Edoran asked. "And if we can, by how much?"

"I was thinking about that." Togger fell silent, then went on, "Yes. The wind's against us, but it'll be against them as well, and blowing stronger on the open strait than in the islands. Their ships are faster than ours, but . . . Lass, before they had to hurry off to Boralee, did they anchor down at night?"

"Yes," Arisa confirmed. "Or sailed a lot slower after nightfall. I don't think they're in a huge hurry now. I know that each part of the fleet plans to wait for the other before they try to raid you."

"We can't count on that delaying them, but it's four days' sailing to Caerfalas from here, so two days and nights. The tide'll turn in just a few hours, so we won't be far behind them. If we sail close in . . . We should beat them home by at least twelve hours, and maybe more. Maybe a lot more, if they have to wait for their comrades, but twelve hours is as certain as anything gets at sea." Relief eased the strain on his weathered face. "That will be long enough for us to get so far inland they won't be able to track us down. We'll lose our boats, but boats might be replaced someday, and lives can't. We'll go to sea in other men's ships for a while."

"Why not escape in the ships?" Arisa asked. "Then you'd have both."

"Too risky," said Togger. "If our boats are gone, they'll come looking for them. Their ships are faster, and armed with cannons, too! No, we have to run inland, no matter the cost. Poor's better than dead."

"You might be able to save the ships," said Edoran, trying to remember the width of the old fortress gate as he swiftly revised his plan. "We *might* even be able to save some of the houses. I've got an idea, but there's a lot of risk involved. I'm not sure it's worth it. You'd have to make that decision."

Togger sighed. "I'll have to gather the others anyway, to tell them we're sailing the moment the tide turns enough for us to launch. And why, bright Lady help us! After you've told your part of the tale, you can tack your plan onto the end of it. We'll see what the others might come up with as well."

He hurried off, and Edoran grimaced. "He didn't take me seriously."

"He didn't laugh in your face, either," said Arisa. Edoran's heart lifted at the familiar tart tone. He should have known that the prospect of action would raise her spirits. "They'll listen," she went on. "If your plan makes sense, they'll think about it. If it doesn't, they'll tell you so. What more do you expect?"

She wasn't taking his plan seriously either, Edoran realized. And like Togger, she knew *him*, not the reputation Pettibone had created. Doubt seized him. If they agreed to his plan, and people died . . .

"I need your help," he told Arisa.

"Good. Are you ready to tell me about this plan of yours?"

"No," said Edoran. "I want you to lay out the cards."

They found a quiet place, down by the beach where the fishing boats awaited the tide. Edoran located another blanket, spread it between them, took the deck Arisa offered him, and shuffled it several times.

"That's enough," said Arisa. "Draw the first card."

"You're the one with all the withe." Edoran handed the deck to her.

She eyed him, considering. "I'm not so sure about that." But she turned the first card anyway.

The fool grinned up at them, and Edoran's shoulders slumped in relief. "That's me. It's working."

Arisa nodded. "Wisdom of the heart," she said. "This supports you."

Edoran braced himself for the swirling vortex of chaos, but the wheel of fortune appeared below the fool. "It's . . . it's different!"

"Different from what?" Arisa asked. "I wouldn't want my plan to rest on fortunes that change."

"No, I think it means that *my* fortune . . . Never mind. Go on."

Arisa laid a card above the fool. "The trial. Judgment of a person or situation; make it wisely."

Edoran sobered. His judgments had often been wrong.

"This misleads you," said Arisa, laying a card at the fool's far right.

"Vacillation." Edoran gazed at the pictured man, torn between two market stalls, with the sun setting behind him. "It always has."

Did this mean he should commit to his plan? Or abandon it? Or simply make up his mind?

"What guides me?" he asked.

Arisa set the hanged man between the vacillation and the fool.

"Weasel?" Edoran asked. "That's his card, isn't it?" How could Weasel guide him? He wasn't even there.

"It is Weasel's card," said Arisa slowly. "But it really indicates voluntary sacrifice, for the greater good. Maybe that's what it means now."

So was he supposed to sacrifice the wealth and comforts of the palace? Or his aching desire to leave them behind, to become nothing but Ron of Caerfalas? Edoran was beginning to understand why Weasel was skeptical of the cards. They were easier to interpret when laid by a Hidden priest, with visions pouring off him like sparks from a fire. He rubbed his forehead, which was beginning to ache. "Go on."

Since chaos had changed, he'd hoped not to see the flaming tower in the threat position, but there it lay. The horror that card had always evoked swept over Edoran. When you were going to rule a kingdom, being threatened with the destruction of everything was terrifying.

Even Arisa had paled. "Are you sure about this plan of yours? If it goes wrong . . . well, it might be important."

"It would be important if it went right, too," said Edoran wearily. "It would be important if it could have worked, but I gave up on it."

Disaster had always threatened him, in one form or another. At least now fortune's wheel offered a chance at escape.

"This protects you," Arisa said, laying the final card between the tower and the fool. Then she gasped.

Edoran gazed down at the goddess walking on storm clouds. "That's you, isn't it? The storm?"

"Yes, and I don't like being between you and the tower." She wrapped her arms around herself, as if warding off a sudden chill. "I don't like it at all."

"But it's also . . . well, a storm," Edoran said. "Creation and destruction in the same package. Like winning a war."

"Every war that someone wins, someone else loses," said Arisa. "That's the point. All waters cards are about things having two sides."

It could also indicate creation from destruction. Like a prince vanishing, and a fisherboy being born. Edoran stared at the wheel, the card that had taken the place of chaos, which only spun to nothing. His fortunes *were* changing.

"I'm going to tell them my plan," he said. "They can make up their own minds."

Arisa gathered up the cards and said nothing.

The fishermen who gathered on the beach near their boats were quiet, oppressed by Boralee's grief. Then Togger told them Arisa's story, which frightened them to near panic. In fact, they refused to believe her till she hiked down the beach and brought the sword and shield back with her.

Edoran, who'd become thoroughly familiar with them even before he'd had to carry them over the countryside, saw only a couple of battered antiques. He'd grown up in a palace full of antiques, most of which were in better condition.

The fishermen of Caerfalas gazed at them in awe. Except for Togger, who folded his arms and snapped, "Come now, it's not having the sword and shield that makes the king; it's him knowing them. You all know that, whatever the townsmen have forgotten. So stop gawking, and give me some thoughts about how we can salvage the most from this mess."

"Salvage?" one of the other boat captains said bitterly. "We'll have time to get home and get our families out—the One God and the Lady be thanked for that! But we can't carry our homes or our boats with us, and if they caught us at sea . . ."

"Well," said Togger, "it occurs to me that not every man needs to go running inland. If there's anyone who'd be willing to stay here with his boat, and trust the rest of us to see his family safe, we could at least save some of them. Is anyone willing to stay here, while the rest of us return to Caerfalas?"

The silence stretched.

"Come now," said Togger. "Surely there's someone you'd trust to watch over your family, along with his own."

"Then why aren't you volunteering?" one of the other men asked.

"Now that's not fair. My children are young, and a handful! I . . . Oh, you're right, you're right. It wouldn't matter how old they were. Even if it was only my wife at risk, I couldn't stand to wait here, knowing they were in danger. It was foolish to think you wouldn't feel the same. But if we all go back, all our ships will be lost. We can find places in other villages, on other men's boats, but Caerfalas will be gone, even if the pirates don't burn it to the ground."

Edoran took a deep breath. "Not necessarily. I've been thinking. It's almost impossible to attack people who have stout walls to defend them. That's why there are so many old fortresses, from the warring time before Deor."

"We know that, lad," said Togger. "But Caerfalas is too big to build a wall around even if we had years, much less twelve hours."

"I can't think of any way to protect the houses," Edoran admitted. His heart was pounding. He wasn't sure if he was more afraid that they'd reject his plan, or that they'd accept it. "But the walls of that abandoned fortress behind the village are still intact, and the space inside is pretty empty. If you could drag the ships in . . . Well, it's a defensible position. You could send all the children and old folks to safety—anyone who couldn't fight. They'd be safe before you started working on the fortress. And if the pirates came before you were ready, since there'd be no one left but young, fit men, you'd be able to outrun them. Especially since you know the countryside around there, and they don't."

They were all staring at him in astonishment. Even Arisa. Edoran felt his face grow warm, and knew he was blushing.

"We've got the logs we use as rollers when we want to beach a boat really high," said one of the men. "It'd take some work to clear the ground between the beach and the fortress, but . . . is that old gate wide enough?"

Togger was rubbing his chin furiously. "If I remember right, it is. But it won't do, lad. Behind those walls we might be able to hold them off for several days, maybe even a few weeks, but then what? There'd always be more of them than of us. It might work in the short run, but we couldn't hold them off for long."

He sounded as if he regretted that, and hope flared in Edoran's heart. "You wouldn't have to hold them long. Just long enough for us to get them talking. If we showed them the sword and shield, and told them we wanted to trade them for our freedom, and the release of the Falcon's hostage . . ."

A babble of voices broke out. "They'd just swarm over the walls and take us! 'Specially with the shield and sword as a prize."

"Not if we threaten to break the sword and shield to bits if they continue their attack," said Edoran firmly. Horror dawned in the faces around him, but he didn't care. The sword and shield were only hunks of metal and wood—it was Weasel, and the people of Caerfalas, who mattered. "They know how much the Falcon wants the sword and shield," he went on. "If we drag out an ax and start chopping bits off the shield, they'd have to break off their attack and send for the Falcon. I'm sure of that."

Almost sure.

"You can't give the sword and shield back to my mother." Arisa looked as aghast as the fishermen. "I stole them to keep them *out* of her hands!"

"If I can trade them for Weasel, I don't care who has them," Edoran said.

"Hold up here," said Togger. "Who's this Weasel you're talking about? What hostage?"

Arisa explained why she'd left the palace in the first place, and who Weasel was. And wasn't. "The shareholders, they'll just write him off," she finished. "A lowborn clerk, with no family. Even Regent Holis, who loves him, wouldn't put the realm in danger for his sake."

"I think . . ." Edoran choked down the rest of the sentence. I *think he wanted to* was something Ron the fisherboy had no way of knowing. "I don't think it matters," he said. "Because if the pirates were captured, and it was proved that the Falcon was behind them, no one would ever accept her as ruler, whether she had the sword and shield or not."

Togger snorted. "That's certainly true. If folk learned she was behind those pirates, she'd be lucky to escape Deorthas alive." Arisa flinched, and he laid a comforting hand on her shoulder. "I'm sorry, lass, but it's the truth. And I can't see it matters much, because even if we could hold the pirates off for a time, there's no way in the world we could capture them! Not to mention the navy sailors with 'em. There are too many of them and too few of us. You're dreaming, Ron."

"Of course you can't capture them," said Edoran. "That's what the guard is for."

There was a moment of silence.

"What guard?" Togger was beginning to sound rattled.

"The guardsmen to whom the people here in Boralee are going to take our letter, explaining that this attack was a diversion, and where the pirates are going next. Look at the timing. The outlying farms will already have sent men to tell the guard about the attack on Boralee. All the troops in the area will be heading this way in a day or so, right?"

"Aye," said Togger. "And they'll get here in just a few more days, which is right when the pirates will be raiding Caerfalas. That's what they're counting on."

"Exactly," Edoran said. "If the Boralee townsfolk sent out messengers to the guard, telling them what was really going on, they'd head for Caerfalas instead. In fact, if they saw a chance to set up an ambush for the pirates, to get ahead of them for once, I bet they'd get to Caerfalas pretty quickly."

They were all listening now. Some were frowning, but hope was beginning to dawn.

"While the guards are gathering," Edoran went on, "we stand off that first attack just long enough to convince the pirates that they have to send for the Falcon and Weasel. They know she wants the sword and shield, so they'll have to send word and get her orders. And I bet she'll come herself. She's like that."

He didn't dare look at Arisa.

"It will take them several more days, maybe a week, to get her and Weasel and come back to Caerfalas. That would give the guards time to arrive. Maybe even bring in reinforcements, and set up a real ambush."

The fishermen's voices rose in such a babble that Edoran couldn't hear what they said, but they seemed to like the idea. Only Togger was scowling.

"There's not enough guards," he said. "Not that could be gathered in time. If the Falcon wants the sword and shield as bad as you say, she'll bring more men with her when she comes for it. Maybe even her whole fleet. And it won't be only the sword and shield she's coming for." He glanced at Arisa, then looked away. "The guards who could come would, and they'd set up their ambush and fight. They might even win. But in a battle where neither side has a clear advantage . . . the death toll would be terrible, lad."

But he hadn't refused outright.

Edoran wiped sweating palms on his britches. "Not if the Falcon surrendered."

"Which she won't! Not as long as she has any chance of winning, or even a chance to fight free. And the odds will likely be in her favor."

"But if her ships were gone, if while she was ashore negotiating with us a handful of men swam out to her ships with slow matches and set fuses to her powder magazines . . . Even if she could outfight the guard, it wouldn't do her any good. Because then she and her men would have to escape on foot, through half the width of Deorthas, with every carter, farmer, and townsman looking for a chance to bring them to justice. They'd never make it. She'd know that. And then, if someone offered the pirates prison instead of the noose, and the Falcon herself exile . . ."

The war between hope and dread in Arisa's face was so terrible, he had to look away.

"She'd have to surrender," he finished. "She'd have no choice, if her ships were gone."

The noise that broke out then was more than liking—it sounded almost like cheers.

"Wait!" Togger shouted. "We have to think about this, rot you! Don't they leave a guard on their ships, when they go raiding ashore?"

"Not on the ship I escaped from." Arisa's face was alight now. "There were two men on deck, but they were both hanging over the rail, watching the shore. It wasn't hard to climb down. I don't think it would be any harder to climb up, if you came up on them from behind."

"*Could* someone swim out to the ships without being seen?" Edoran asked. That was the part of his plan he had the most doubts about.

"Depends on the light," said Togger. "If it's night, there'd be no trouble, even with a moon. If there's rain or fog, probably. If it's bright day, and the lookouts are at all alert, it'd be impossible."

Edoran extended his weather sensing. It would rain the day after tomorrow, but then turn fair again for the next few days. So unless the pirates arrived at night, his plan would fail.

"Not impossible," another man protested. "Just . . . Oh, all right, if the lookouts were watching, they'd get caught."

"So we'll have to make sure everyone's watching the shore," another put in. "Like they were when Arisa here went over the side."

The discussion that broke out then was about "how" and "when" and "first we'll have to." No one asked, *Should we? Not* even Togger or Arisa. But the dread lingered in Edoran's heart. They'd all agreed to this plan, but if anything went wrong and someone died, it would be his fault. And if he hadn't put forward his plan, and they'd lost everything, would that have been his fault too? Edoran sighed.

The letters to the guard, the explanations to Boralee's townsfolk, were complicated enough that the fishermen were several hours late launching the boats, though the launching went far more swiftly with all of Boralee's citizens on the ropes.

Walking into the town to talk to the council had been like walking into a fog of grief and fury, so intense that Edoran had to struggle to act normally. Arisa turned pale and silent once more. The bodies had been removed, but their blood still stained the stones. Edoran, trying to pay attention to a discussion between Togger, the head councilman, and a stable master who owned several fast horses, stepped into one such puddle and almost fell as the shock of recent death reverberated from the earth.

The stable master volunteered his horses to carry the messages and offered to ride one himself. All of Boralee was ready to do anything they could to get back at the men who'd taken so much from them. The boats were launched with their crews aboard—only a handful of fishermen even got their feet wet.

It was better at sea, for the water held no lingering trauma, and the fresh wind might have been designed to blow away doubts. Still, Edoran volunteered to take the first night shift, since he didn't think he could sleep.

Judging by the worried faces around him, no one was going to sleep well that night. But it was Arisa who came up to him as he stared out over the rolling waves, hoping he could spot a half-submerged log in time to warn the helmsman about it. Even in the moonlight, it didn't seem likely.

Arisa settled her arms on the railing beside him, gazing at the sea. "It's too risky. It's probably my mother's best chance to get out of this alive, but it's too complicated. It depends on perfect timing by everyone involved—most of whom are your enemies! There's just too much that can go wrong."

"I know," said Edoran. "But we have to do something. This is the only way I can think of to get Weasel out of your mother's hands, and to save both the people of Caerfalas and their village."

"The village will almost certainly burn," Arisa told him. "Before the pirates even find the fortress."

"The village is their boats, not their houses," said Edoran. "I've been here long enough to know that much."

This plan was also his best chance to keep the Falcon alive, for her daughter's sake. If the Falcon surrendered, Arisa would go into exile with her. Edoran would miss her more than he'd have believed possible a few months ago. He'd learned to rely on Weasel's judgment, but her fiery desire to make things right challenged him to do the same. Or at least to modify her plans so that they might work, instead of heading straight for disaster.

And she must be influencing him more than he'd realized, for he'd come up with this plan all on his own.

If the Falcon did choose to fight and die, at least he could keep her daughter safe. She would heal, eventually. But even knowing how much he'd miss Arisa, he *really* hoped the Falcon chose to surrender. She'd have to surrender if her ships were destroyed. Wouldn't she? Edoran sighed.

"There's another problem you may not have considered," Arisa went on. "Suppose she lights a fuse and throws a couple of kegs of gunpowder into the fortress. Then she could storm the walls and pull the sword and shield out of the wreckage. They might well survive that kind of damage, but your fishermen won't."

He could see how much it cost her to admit that her mother might do such a thing, but she'd found the courage to warn him. The least he could do was offer her the whole truth in return.

"If she brings up kegs of gunpowder, I'll step in myself," said Edoran. "Once she knows I'm behind those walls, there won't be any powder kegs going over them."

"I thought about that," said Arisa. "But once she knows you're there, she has to take you. You, alive in her hands, is her only chance to come out on top of this mess. That's what Weasel got himself kidnapped to prevent!"

She slammed her fists on the railing in frustration. Edoran was grateful that she so seldom cried.

"Preventing her from taking the fortress is what the guards are for," Edoran reminded her.

"If they get there in time. Too risky. Too complex. Something is bound to go wrong."

It was time. "I'm counting on complex," said Edoran. "I'm counting on chaos, and confusion, and nobody knowing what's going on. Because somewhere in all that confusion, I'm going to find a way for Prince Edoran to die."

He'd hoped to startle her with that statement, but she didn't even look away from the waves. "So that's it. I wondered what you were up to. Why you wouldn't let me tell people who you are. You're going to stay here, aren't you? To run away from your duty to your people. From the debt you owe Justice Holis. You plan to take the coward's way out."

"You were just accusing me of taking too much risk!" He'd known she'd think that, but it still stung.

"That's different. That's risking yourself for the people of Caerfalas, and it's kind of noble even if it is a stupid plan. This is just running."

"You're right," said Edoran. He couldn't even claim he was choosing a more dangerous life, for the palace had never held safety for him. Pettibone had murdered a king to make himself regent. Ron the fisherboy would be safer than Prince Edoran had ever been. Well, except for pirates. And storms. And the kind of accidents that could always happen when men worked with ropes, and swinging booms, and sharp knives. Weasel's father had been killed by a falling crate.

"It's not about safety," Edoran told her. "It's not even about cowardice, really. It's about . . ." Happiness. The freedom to make a life for himself, where he could be happy. Was that so wrong? "Never mind."

"Well, I don't want my mother blamed for your death," Arisa told him. "That would get her hanged for sure."

"Agreed," said Edoran. "If anyone was going to hang for it, of course I'd step forward. But surely there will be a chance for some accident. I could simply vanish. You could swear you saw me fall off the wall, or . . . or something."

It was hard to think of a plausible accident. He could always be killed in battle, but he was hoping there wouldn't be any battle. And if he was slain in the fighting, or fell off the wall, then where was his corpse? This dying thing was harder than it sounded. Still . . .

"I never wanted to be king," Edoran said. "Pettibone made it pretty clear I never would be, but even when I imagined proving my father's murder and seeing him hang, I didn't want to become king at the end of it. I'd be bad at it too. Whoever Holis chooses will do better, and be happier with the job. Maybe you could say you saw me drown? That'd explain why there's no body."

Arisa snorted. "I could say I saw you run mad—and that would be true!"

"But I'd be a terrible king. And you know it."

"Actually, I'm not sure about that," Arisa said. "Though I have to admit, I'm kind of surprised by it."

It was Edoran's turn to snort. "Name one thing I've done, in all my life, that makes you think I should be king."

"You came up with this plan," said Arisa. "It's not perfect, but

you're trying to save everything that really matters. Your priori-
ties are right."

"You said it was a stupid plan!"

"It is. And it rests on all the fisherfolk being willing to trust the
daughter of a traitor, which is downright crazy."

"But they can trust you," Edoran said. "They *are* trusting you.
Right now."

"Do you know why?" Arisa asked him.

Edoran blinked. "Because you're telling the truth."

"No, you blockhead! They're trusting me because you told
them they could! They're trusting you. Your Highness."

She left him then, so he could think it over. So he could think
about all that could fail, and the responsibility for that failure sitting squarely on his shoulders.

This was what it meant to be king. Only all the time. And she
thought he should want that job? She was crazy!

The chaotic mess his so-clever plan was bound to produce was
the best chance to vanish he was ever likely to get. By all the gods,
he'd take it!

CHAPTER 11

THE TOWER

*The Tower: ultimate destruction, not of you,
but of your world. The loss of all you hold dear.*

The wind was against them. They arrived at Caerfalas at midmorning of the day Togger had hoped to arrive before dawn—the day he thought the pirates would arrive at dusk. But the wind would be against the pirates, too, Edoran thought, as they rammed the boats up onto the shore and splashed through the surf. So the pirates might arrive late as well. Or tomorrow, if they wanted light for their raid on the village. Or even the next day, if their comrades were delayed.

But now or later, they would come. He knew Arisa too well to doubt that—and the fisherfolk of Caerfalas were trusting his word for it.

The men brought their families to the meeting hall. Then they left them to listen to Togger, Arisa, and Edoran, while they went home to pack up food and any small, valuable items the women and older children could carry.

The women, who hadn't seen Boralee burning, were less inclined to take the threat seriously. Arisa had to tell her whole story, in detail, before they were willing to believe her.

Then Edoran told them his plan. At first they thought it was ridiculous, but the more he explained, the more thoughtful they became. He was talking about some of the ways they might keep the ships' watchmen's attention fixed on the shore when Moll held up a hand for silence.

"I still think the lot of you might be spooking at shadows," she said. "Though those pirates suddenly raiding ashore always seemed odd. Maybe the Falcon trying to make Holis look bad explains it. And maybe it doesn't. But if you're wrong, all it'll cost us is a few days' work. If the raid doesn't come, that's all we've lost. I've been planning to visit my cousin in Falter; now's probably the time. And if you're right and the raid does come, then your plan might save our boats. That's worth some risk."

The women scattered then, to go home and repack the things their men had packed already.

"Will they get our messages to the guard fast enough?" Edoran fretted. "We're going to need all the troops we can get, not just the ones near Boralee. They don't seem to be taking this seriously!"

"I'm not worried about that," said Togger. "There's a handful of girls, a bit older than you are now, but when they were your age they were crazy for horses. We've nothing larger than donkeys here, but a lot of the nearby farms have plow horses, and they all learned to ride. If we give them a chance to play hero on horse-back, they'll take it seriously. Better than a boy that age, 'cause they're less likely to break their necks showing off.

"I wrote the letters while we were sailing," Togger went on. "We can send them off right now. I want you two to examine that old fortress. Figure out what we need to do to make it defensible, and what tools and supplies we'll need. And while you're at it, take a string and measure that gate! No good pulling boats all the way up there if they can't pass through when they arrive."

Arisa waited till he was out of sight before turning to Edoran. "I don't know anything about defending a fortress. All I ever learned about was robbing coaches and avoiding the law."

"Why didn't you tell Togger that?" Edoran asked.

"Because these people need all the confidence they can get," said Arisa. "If they think we know what we're talking about, it might help almost as much as us actually knowing."

Edoran could feel the blood drain from his face. "I don't know anything about any kind of fighting. I've never been in a real fight in my life. You know that!"

"Well, I have," said Arisa. "And you do know things about fighting in a fortress, because you've been telling us about it for the past three days!"

"That's just what I read in my father's journals," Edoran hissed. *She* was supposed to be the expert. "And he'd never done it either! He liked history, so he wrote about things like that. That's all!"

"Then maybe between us we can figure things out," said Arisa. "Because one thing I know about real fights is that if people think they're going to lose, they *will* lose. Let's go look at this place, and try to find a way they can win!"

For all her brave words, Edoran could tell she was worried. When they rounded the last of the low hills that lay between the fortress and the village, and she saw the walls, her eyes widened. "It's a real fortress!"

"You were expecting painted cloth, like the players use?" Edoran asked.

"Well no, but . . . I'm going to walk around the walls. If they're all in such good shape . . ."

She went off, gazing first up at the walls, then at the landscape around them, and muttering to herself. Edoran found that encouraging.

He had followed enough children on their games to know the terrain fairly well, so he went through the gate and stood looking around, with what his father had written about sieges in his mind. What he saw depressed him.

"I can tell you one thing," said Arisa when she finally followed him inside. "No one is getting over that wall without a rope or a ladder. And you can't fight if you're climbing. None of the nearby hills is taller than this, so they can't shoot down on us either. If you had enough people to cut ropes and push down ladders, you could defend these walls forever!"

"But they have to be able to reach them," said Edoran glumly.

"What?"

"In order to push down ladders and things, people have to be standing on a walkway that lets them reach the top of the wall from the inside—and that walkway rotted a long time ago. We knew we'd have to build a new gate, but a walkway is going to be a lot more work."

Some of the enthusiasm faded from Arisa's face, but she said firmly, "They'll just have to build it."

"Will they have time?" Edoran asked.

"Do I look like a carpenter? Let's go tell Togger what we found, and maybe he'll know."

The good news was that the gate was even wider than Edoran remembered.

Togger had already thought of the need to build a walkway around the inside of the walls. "We've timber enough," he said. "As to whether there's time, that depends on how fast the pirates are. But first we have to get the ships inside, or there won't be any reason to build anything."

The woman and children had already departed, all those who were going. Moll headed up a cadre of woman who were young and strong, or old and still strong—or at least too stubborn to flee.

"I thought you were going to visit your cousin," Togger grumbled at her. "You know my wife needs help controlling those boys."

Moll snorted. "Your wife could whip twice the number she's got into line, and make them wash behind their ears besides. My cousin's waited this long, she'll wait a bit longer. And I'll have a better tale to tell when I see her too."

Togger sighed. "I can't make you go. But I'd rather you were safe."

"I'd like us all to stay safe," said Moll tartly. "So we'd best set about it."

"I've read," Edoran said cautiously, "that in the old days women helped in sieges. They threw stones, and heated pitch to pour down on the attackers."

"We don't have much pitch," Togger said. "We all caulked our hulls before we set sail, and we haven't had time to replenish our supply."

Moll snorted. "And you thought you didn't need us! Fish oil, you fool. Heat that to boiling, and it'll scald a man's hide right off. Which should do a pretty fair job of discouraging the folks around him too!"

The image of sheets of searing oil descending onto a man's skin flashed into Edoran's mind. He prayed they wouldn't have to use it, even on pirates.

The next job, for the whole village, was to get their boats into the fortress. Togger said that the measurement Edoran and Arisa had reported would easily admit the smaller boats, and maybe the larger ones. Edoran had thought they'd start pulling the boats in immediately, but he soon learned that the preparations for dragging the boats to the fortress would take almost as long as the task itself. First they had to clear a path to the fortress gate. Even following the old roadbed, which was relatively flat, they had to deal with rocks that had tumbled down onto it, and centuries of plant growth. Few trees grew so near the sea, but some of the scrubby bushes were almost as tall, and their trunks were incredibly tough.

The village already possessed the logs they needed for rollers, and having helped pull the boats over the sand, Edoran had assumed that dragging them around on rollers would be easier. It wasn't.

By the time the first boat approached the fortress gate his hands were blistered, his muscles ached, and sweat was pouring into his eyes. And worse, Togger had begun to eye the horizon for approaching sails.

By the time they got the last of the boats inside it was full dark, his blisters had broken, and Edoran was so tired he didn't care if the pirates came or not. Some of the boats were tall enough for a man standing on them to see over the wall, but they weren't tall enough to form the walkway the fishermen needed. They hadn't even built a new gate yet.

He summoned the last of his strength and climbed the ladder to the tallest boat, which Togger was using as a scouting platform. "It's still not defensible," Edoran told the fisherman. "In fact, it's . . . it's . . ."

"'Death trap' is the word you're looking for," said Arisa, following him up the ladder. She didn't look nearly as tired as Edoran felt, curse her.

"That makes no difference now," said Togger. He had climbed onto the railing to get a better view. "The good news is that there's enough moonlight that I'd be able to see their sails if they were coming. I think we're safe till morning, and that's a good thing, for we've none of us the energy to fight a kitten."

"So what do we do?" Edoran was almost too tired to care about the answer.

"We set a watch," said Togger. "If they show up tonight, we run. But I'm betting they won't. They'll want light, sailing up to a strange beach. After a night's sleep we'll build a gate, and then see what we can do to make this place a real fortress!"

They rose at dawn and set about building a new gate and walkway around the inside wall. The men of the village were accustomed to working together on carpentry projects, building sheds or even a new house in a few days. And the need to repair their boats meant they had plenty of wood on hand. This was a task about which neither Edoran nor Arisa knew anything, so they helped Moll and the other women bring their larger valuables from their homes to store inside the boats—beginning with food stores, so they'd be able to eat if the siege lasted for more than a few days. And bedding so they could sleep warm, and fuel for cook fires and to heat pitch and fish oil.

They all worked with the understanding that if the scouts who were watching for sails shouted a warning before the gate and walkway were completed, everyone would drop what they were doing and run for the low hills behind the village. Until those tasks were complete, the fortress was nothing but the death trap Arisa had called it.

Edoran worked through the morning expecting that shout any minute. By afternoon he was looking for sails himself, whenever the sea was in his sight. Walking down the now well-trodden path to the fortress, he was looking over his shoulder when he tripped and almost dropped the spinning wheel he was carrying.

"Watch what you're about!" Moll snapped. "That was built by Aggie's great-grandfather, and it's got the smoothest spin I've ever seen. She'll be right miffed if you break it."

"But where are they?" Edoran demanded.

"I don't know." Moll's voice was more gentle now. "We can't know what might delay them, or for how long. Our task is to make use of all the time they give us, so leave the scouts to their job, and you get on with yours."

By nightfall the gate and walkway were finished, and the men had gathered everything in the village that could be used as a weapon. The women had prepared a meal, which everyone ate in near silence. Arisa was standing on the wall, staring out to sea, when Edoran went to sleep in a warm bedroll on a comfortable pallet. He slept badly.

The next morning the men made pens for their livestock in one corner, and brought in the cows, sheep, chickens, and pigs, and their feed as well.

The women worked out who would sleep in what boat if it rained. Edoran thought about what would happen if someone on the other side of the wall set fire to those boats, and soon all the men were down on the beach shoveling sand into any container that couldn't hold water. The barrels, flasks, and kegs that could hold water were already full.

"It took me two days to realize they could roast us like geese in an oven," Edoran fretted to Arisa. "What else have I missed?"

They worked with the young men who were to hide in the hills and ultimately swim out to blow up the pirate ships— though the burning slow match of Edoran's imagining had been replaced with a striker.

"How could I keep a slow match alight in the water?" Mouse had pointed out. He'd been chosen as one of the swimmers, and he hadn't even tried to conceal his pride and excitement. He thought this was an adventure, and Edoran wanted to swear at him every time the subject came up. He could swim too! But Togger had refused to even consider Edoran swimming out to the ships.

They'd also checked out how well the swimmers could see the fortress from their hiding places, and rejected any subtle signals such as scratching a nose or tugging an ear. The only things the swimmers were certain to see were big, obvious gestures, such as waving an arm back and forth—which would be obvious to the watching pirates as well. They'd finally settled for someone thrusting a fist into the air, one time for every half hour to be set on the fuses.

Then Arisa had to explain to the swimmers how many feet per half hour, with the several different kinds of fuses they were likely to find, which didn't reassure Edoran at all.

But the amount of time they'd need to set on the fuses would depend on how the situation at the fortress developed—if nothing else, they didn't dare risk blowing up the ships while Weasel was still aboard. And Edoran had been selected to give the signal, since Togger said that a man of his years waving his fists around like a schoolboy would look peculiar—particularly if it happened in the middle of negotiations.

One thrust for each half hour of fuse, Edoran chanted to himself, wondering how he would have any idea how much time to ask for. Half an hour was the minimum, for they had to allow the swimmers time to escape. At least all the pirates would have plenty of powder and fuses, because they carried—

"Cannons!" Edoran grabbed Arisa's arm and lowered his voice

from the near yelp he'd used. "What will happen if the pirates bring their cannons ashore to break the walls?"

"We'll probably die," said Arisa. "Because this fortress wasn't built to withstand cannon fire. But I doubt they'll try that before your swimmers blow up the ships. Cannons are hard to take apart and reassemble, and it's tricky to get them into a small boat to row ashore. And when they first land, they won't know that they might need them."

If someone was rowing back to his ship to arrange for the cannons when the swimmers were in the water . . .

"They're not my swimmers," Edoran snapped. "I wish I'd never thought about using the fortress. This is too cursed complicated!"

"I told you that in the first place," said Arisa. "But one thing is about to go right."

"What?"

She pointed toward the village. "Unless I'm seeing things, that's a guard troop!"

Edoran spun, gazing eagerly into the distance at the green and white uniforms and the horses' shining tack. He'd never seen anything more beautiful in his life, but . . .

"There are only twenty of them!"

Soon there were fewer. Once he'd heard the complete story, the troop's captain sent half a dozen men galloping off to bring back reinforcements. Edoran eyed the remaining fourteen gloomily.

"Needless to say, we can't do much for you ourselves," the captain apologized. "But any other troops your messengers find will soon be on their way, and my men know where to look for them! If your plan to delay the pirates in negotiation works, by the time they return with their leader we should be assembled in force."

He politely declined to bring the few men he had into the fortress, claiming that if the pirates encountered trained fighters on the walls, they might become suspicious.

Accustomed to the language of courtiers, Edoran easily translated this to I *think you're going to get slaughtered the moment the pirates come at your silly wall.*

Judging by his scowl, Togger understood it as well, but there was nothing he could do about it.

Edoran went to sleep that night torn between praying that the pirates never came and realizing how furious the whole village would be with him if all of this had been for nothing.

But when Arisa shook him awake, shortly after dawn, the pirates had come.

"They've counted eight ships," she told Edoran as he scrambled up the ladder to the walkway. "I think the pirates only had about eight ships originally, though now they've added three navy ships to their fleet."

"If I'm any judge of sails, three of those ships in the bay used to be navy," said Togger. He sounded calmer than Edoran felt, but his face was pale under winter's light tan. "If your count's right, lass, they sent more than two-thirds of their fleet to deal with little Caerfalas. I think that's flattering!"

The villagers' laughter was almost a cheer, but Edoran didn't join in. He wasn't sure how many pirates eight ships could hold, but it was going to be more than he'd expected. A lot more.

Not all the ships launched their crews at once—only the five that Togger had identified as pirate vessels lowered their longboats, which then started rowing for the shore. Four boats per ship, each holding eight to ten men . . . almost two hundred pirates raced up the beach toward the silent, empty houses. Homes, Edoran corrected himself, watching Moll wince at the distant crash of breaking glass.

"Curse the scum," she muttered under her breath. "They know how hard those windows are to replace."

Edoran frowned. "How would pirates know about replacing windows?"

The tense misery on her face eased into anger. "Where do you think those men came from, Ron? Or merchant seamen, or naval sailors? Life at sea's not something a man's likely to choose unless he's born to it. Those . . . *men*, they were born in villages just like ours. They know right well how much replacing that glass will cost! Of course, they intend to kill us all, so maybe they're thinking it won't matter."

Edoran frowned, astonished. "If they come from a village like this, how could they . . . ?"

Moll shrugged. "In any group of humans there's always a few who are rotten. Just the nature of folks, I guess. It's the men hiding in those navy ships, who've turned their dogs loose on us and then turned their backs, who bother me. They, the common seamen, not the officers, they're from the villages too. They were good men once. Or supposed to be, Udan seize their black hearts."

"I don't understand," Edoran whispered. How could someone who came from a place like Caerfalas be willing to do what those men were doing—or would do, if they could break the fortress walls? How could any men, no matter where they came from?

"I do understand," said Arisa. "My mother had a few like that among her men. Most were fighting for a cause they believed in, but not all."

A kettle of simmering oil sat on the walkway beside her, and Arisa had a dipper in her hand. She'd sworn to Togger that she'd be able to use it, and Edoran hadn't understood that, either. Now, looking at the faces of the villagers around him as smoke began to rise from their homes, he was beginning to.

Edoran had been given a pole to push down ladders—and Arisa had pointed out he could whack men over the head with it. At the time he'd been a little offended at not receiving a real weapon. Now he resolved to use it well.

The road up to the fortress was so plainly marked that Edoran was surprised it took the pirates even a handful of minutes to find it, but soon they appeared, walking swiftly up the trail. When they saw the fortress they stopped, scowling in a way that was almost comical.

Edoran stared at them. He didn't know what he'd expected, but it was something more villainous than these ordinary-looking sailors. More of them were clean shaven than the Caerfalas fishermen had been at sea! Had he passed them in a market square,

Edoran wouldn't have looked at any of their weather-beaten faces and known that this man or that was a killer. Something like that ought to show!

The only thing that marked their intentions was the number of weapons they carried.

Suddenly almost a dozen men lifted their pistols. Edoran dropped to his knees on the walkway just as the shots boomed out. He flinched at the crack of bullets on stone, though he knew those were the ones that had missed. His heart hammered. He wanted to retreat to the darkest corner of some boat's hold and pull blankets over his head. Which would be a dandy position to be in if the pirates broke into the fortress and set the boats on fire.

When Togger rose to his feet and peered cautiously over the wall, Edoran forced his wobbling knees to move and joined him.

The pirates had gathered into small groups and were discussing the matter, with many gestures. And swearing, Edoran hoped. They were better armed than the fishermen; almost half of them had pistols in their belts, and the rest carried cudgels or knives. Many had more than one knife, some of which were almost as long as short swords.

The fishermen's motley armament suddenly seemed weaker. Their gutting knives were short, and there were no pistols in the village, only a couple of scatterguns their owners used for hunting birds.

Arisa had said that a man who could hit a wood dove in flight could certainly hit a man on a ladder, and that the boat hooks with which most of the men were armed were the best possible weapons to defend a wall. They had a longer reach than a knife, a hook that could unseat a ladder, and a point sharp enough to stab a man's hand or put out his eye. And the men were accustomed to handling them, if not fighting with them, which Arisa thought was important.

She'd asked if anyone had a pistol she could borrow and was disappointed when the answer was no. Edoran had pointed out that her knife was bigger than any of the others anyway. Arisa had replied that if the pirates got into knife range, they'd all end up dead.

"We want to negotiate with your leader," Togger called out. "We want to talk to the Falcon about an exchange. We've got the shield of stars and the sword of waters here with us, and we'll trade 'em for the hostage she holds. But we've got to talk to her about it."

They had all agreed on that—no bargains with anyone but the Falcon. The pirates might make promises, but they weren't likely to keep them, and Arisa swore her mother would. Edoran wished he could be certain of that.

The pirates looked at Togger for a moment, but no questions came back, no demands.

"Aren't they going to ask, 'What hostage'?" Edoran said.

"They don't care about that yet," Togger murmured. "They can't leave without trying to take us, but they can't figure out . . . Ah, there they go now."

Almost two-thirds of the pirates jogged off toward the village.

The remainder spread out to encircle the fortress, examining the walls all the way around. Edoran eyed them nervously. They looked more dangerous after that first fusillade than they had before.

A few more shots were fired, but it proved easy to duck behind the wall as soon as a pistol was raised. And all the fishermen were paying close attention.

Edoran soon realized that it would be almost impossible for the pirates, shooting up at an angle, to hit a target as small as a man's face. The closer they came to the wall, the worse the angle grew. His heartbeat began to slow. These walls would keep them safe until—

"Here it comes." Togger's hands tightened on his boat hook.

Looking down the road, Edoran saw that the returning pirates carried nine makeshift ladders.

The villagers had brought all their own ladders inside the fortress, to give them access to the boat decks and walkways. These were made of bits of lumber nailed roughly together, sometimes even bound with rope, but they looked sturdy enough. Edoran reached down and picked up his pole, praying it wouldn't slip in his sweaty hands. His mouth was dry and his legs shook . . . but oddly enough, his stomach was quiet.

He took heart from that, even as the pirates roared a challenge and charged.

Arisa had speculated about the tactics they might use, but all nine ladders slapped upright against the front wall of the fortress. Not a bad idea, for the fishermen didn't dare leave the back and sides completely unguarded. One ladder hit the wall a few feet from Edoran. He took his pole, found a crevice in the looping rope that bound the top step to the brace, and pushed. It was heavier than he'd expected with a man's weight on the bottom, but he braced his feet and put his back into it, and the ladder began to scrape along the stones . . . and then it fell.

Edoran's cheer emerged as a breathless squeak, but he felt better for it.

He looked around for something else to do and saw that two men were moving up the ladder on Arisa's far side, and she was dropping heavy stones down on them. He joined her, and between them they managed to knock the top man off, allowing a couple of fishermen with boat hooks to push the ladder over.

Togger, struggling to push another ladder by himself, shouted for help, and Edoran snatched up his pole while Arisa lifted another stone. A pistol shot sent chips splattering from the edge of the wall as Edoran stood, but none hit him, and there was no time for fear. This was the same ladder he'd pushed down last time, and Edoran's pole found the same crevice and dug in. With him and Togger working together it went over much more easily, and he grinned.

"If we had a few more men," Arisa panted, "we could wait till they were on top of the ladders and then push them down. But I'm afraid if we let them get close to the top, some of them might make it over."

"This wall's almost twenty feet high," Edoran protested without thinking. "Falling that far could kill them!"

He had already started to blush when Arisa replied, "That's the point, moron."

But she didn't sound like she meant it.

"If that's the point, then why are you throwing stones instead of hot oil?"

"Because we're going to have to negotiate with these men, to get them to send for my mother," said Arisa. "And men who've been burned don't usually feel cooperative."

"You think breaking their bones falling will make them more—"

"Pay attention," Togger commanded. "They're ready for another go."

Edoran helped push down three more ladders and hurled several stones. His aim was getting better when one of the pirates shouted an order, and they all withdrew beyond range of the scatterguns.

Edoran looked around. One of the fishermen had cuts on his face from flying stone chips, but he wasn't badly injured. Aside from that, Edoran couldn't see any wounded, much less dead. The pirates, some of whom were limping or clutching their shoulders, had gotten the worst of it.

Togger was grinning. "This fortress of yours was a fine idea, lad!"

"It's not my fortress." Edoran wished he could disavow the idea. This was only the first assault. Next time the pirates might try something that would be harder to deal with. They had to convince them to go for the Falcon and Weasel. They had to get them to leave for several days, to give more guardsmen time to arrive.

The first troop had come in yesterday; surely the others would get here soon.

"Call them again," Edoran told Togger. "Tell them if the sword and shield are lost, the Falcon will . . ."

But it was too late. The pirates were withdrawing, leaving only a handful of scouts to watch . . . their prisoners, Edoran feared. For this fortress was a prison as well.

A few minutes later one of the longboats rowed away from the shore, headed back toward the anchored ships.

"Going to take our message to the Falcon?" Edoran asked. They'd given up awfully easily.

"More likely going to fetch more men," said Arisa. "And real ladders."

Her guess seemed to be right, for the longboat rowed out to one of the navy ships. The debate must have taken awhile— almost an hour later several people climbed down to the longboat, and the rest of the naval ships launched their crews toward the beach.

"Another hundred men, I make it," Togger said, squinting into the distance. "It could be worse."

Edoran hadn't seen any ladders lowered into the boats. If it was just a few more than they'd defeated last time . . . "Maybe the naval officers will be more willing to go get their leader," he said.

Arisa, her gaze fixed on the sea, was silent.

They reached the shore and climbed out of the boats. Some

of the men still wore the blue coats of naval officers, and Edoran scowled at them. Moll was right: They were worse than the pirates. Then the last boat emptied its passengers onto the beach. One of them was much shorter than the others.

Edoran's heart began to pound. Impossible! They'd only learned they needed Weasel a few hours ago.

But when they walked around the curve of the road, it *was* Weasel. And the Falcon walked beside him.

Arisa gasped, but Edoran was too frozen with shock to even do that. She wasn't supposed to be here for another two days! There weren't enough guardsmen to capture all these pirates.

"I told you so," Arisa muttered. "I told you something would go wrong. But if we destroy the ships, she'll still be forced to surrender. They can't make it through the countryside. Well, a handful might. My mother could. But the pirates will be broken!"

"I take it that woman's your mother, lass?" Togger's voice was both cool and gentle. He didn't seem to be impressed by her beauty, either, perhaps the first man Edoran knew who wasn't. Of course, it was hard to appreciate a beautiful woman who was coming to kill you.

"If we destroy the ships, they might storm the fortress for revenge," Edoran said. "They won't have anything to lose then." Or would they? They might all think that they'd be among the handful who'd survive. The fortress had proved more defensible than Edoran expected. It might take them a long time to overcome it. If the fishermen told the pirates that the guard had been summoned, that they were due to arrive any minute—which they were, curse them!—would that speed the pirates on their way?

If he told them the truth while they still had ships to escape in, the pirates would certainly want to run, but would the Falcon let them?

She also wore the blue uniform jacket and white britches of a naval officer, though as she drew nearer Edoran saw they'd been stripped of rank marks. No naval ranking high enough for regent-to-be, he supposed.

Weasel, stumbling behind her in the grip of a couple of officers, wore dirty rags, which Edoran recognized as the remains of the white costume he'd been kidnapped in. His wrists were tied behind him and one eye was still swollen, though the bruises around it were fading to yellow and green.

The officers marched resolutely, but looking at the common sailors who followed them, Edoran saw them eyeing the pirates with distaste, even with dismay. Why hadn't the naval seamen joined that first wave of invaders? Had some of them objected to slaughtering helpless fisherfolk?

The Falcon stopped, just out of gun range, and the men holding Weasel dragged him to a stop as well. Weasel glared at them and said something that earned him a cuff. Remembering the sharpness of his friend's tongue, Edoran wasn't surprised. He'd probably been pricking those men for days. Edoran's spirits rose, in spite of his worries . . . well, terror too. Weasel's spirit hadn't been broken. Edoran's job was to get him safely behind these thick walls, while his body was still in one piece as well.

"I've heard your demands," the Falcon announced clearly.

"And I've come as you asked. Now it's my turn. You're going to send Prince Edoran, the sword and shield, and my daughter out to me now, and I'll leave you all alive."

Edoran glanced at Arisa, wondering if she'd noticed she ranked last in the Falcon's list. Her face was as white and set as marble, but something behind it was crumbling, and his heart flinched in pity.

"If you don't send them out, all of them," the Falcon went on, "I'll cut this boy to pieces in front of you. Then we'll take that foolish fortress apart, and you with it."

"But we don't have . . . ," Togger muttered. Then he raised his voice to a shout. "We don't have Prince Edoran! The sword and shield, aye, and your girl who brought 'em to us. And who we'll not turn out unless she wants to go. But there's no prince here."

A man who wore no uniform pushed forward, and Edoran gasped as he recognized Master Giles.

"This gives you lie!" The fencing master held out a small tan disc. A button. Edoran swore under his breath. The button he'd traded the peddler for candy. Giles must have encountered the peddler—not impossible if he'd spent the past six weeks trying to track the prince. But Edoran would have been at sea when he found it, so he'd sold the information to the highest bidder.

"She will." Arisa's voice was only a whisper. "She'll start cutting Weasel up if you don't give her what she wants. She has to. She'll lose control of those cursed pirates if she looks weak. But you can't go, Your Highness. You can't!"

Edoran's heart began to race. "Why not? If we time it right,

Weasel will be tucked safe in the fortress, and I can swim. Can you swim?"

Arisa's eyes widened. "You're going to get on those ships after the fuses are lit? That's madness! We'll both be killed!"

"*Can you swim?*" Edoran demanded.

She nodded.

"Lad," said Togger, "I don't know who you may be, and right now I don't much care. If you're on those ships when they blow, you *will* be killed."

"Not necessarily," Edoran said. "Almost a dozen sailors survived the explosion on the *Protector*."

"Yes, but—"

"I'm not going to give you all day to discuss it," the Falcon called. "Send them out now, or I start cutting."

"Don't!" Weasel shouted. "It's—"

The officer who held him cuffed him into silence, a much harder blow than the first had been.

"What's the safest place on a ship if the powder blows?" Edoran asked Togger.

"Well, on deck, as far forward as you could get. The powder's going t' be deep in the hold, and likely a bit aft. But no place on that ship will be safe!"

"It's our best chance," said Edoran. "And what better way for . . . What better idea do you have? Watch while she cuts Weasel into collops?"

He met Arisa's eyes and saw her finish the sentence he'd abandoned. *What better way for Prince Edoran to die?*

Edoran scrambled to the top of the wall and stood, revealing himself for all to see. He was the one person there no one wanted to shoot.

"I am Prince Edoran," he announced. "And if my friend is harmed, I'll have you hunted to the far ends of Deorthas and hanged to the last man!"

For emphasis, he thrust both fists into the air.

CHAPTER 12

THE F∞L

The Fool: wisdom of the heart.

The Falcon stared at his raised fists, and Edoran lowered them. He probably looked as ridiculous as he felt, but the signal had been sent. One hour. He had to stall for one hour. More, for it would take the swimmers time to reach the ships, climb aboard, and locate the powder store. An hour and a half? Two hours? And they had to create a diversion, to keep any watchers on the ships focused on the shore.

This was too complicated!

"What are your demands?" Edoran tried to sound regal and dignified, and not as if he'd been too stupid to understand the Falcon the first time.

Her brows rose. "I want you, the shield and sword, and Arisa, all sent out to me. In exchange I'll give you Weasel, and he can go inside the fortress. Which we'll leave intact, with all its defenders alive. If I have you, and the sword and shield, I don't need to kill anyone."

"You send Weasel to the gate," Edoran countered. "Once he's inside, we'll throw the sword and shield down to you. That's an excellent trade for a lowborn clerk, who no one else will even bargain for."

If he gave in too soon, she'd become suspicious. If he stalled too long, the boats might blow up before they got there, and with

Edoran and the sword and shield in her hands, she might end up ruling Deorthas after all.

Too complex. Madness, just as Arisa had said. Even if he surrendered himself with perfect timing, would the Falcon keep her word to leave Weasel and the fisherfolk alive? All those witnesses?

"Are you really prepared to stand there and watch me cut bits off your friend?" The Falcon's voice sounded almost lazy, like the purr of a big lion, and Arisa shivered. She meant it, Edoran realized.

"Are you prepared to watch us cut bits off the shield of stars? I can have it, and an ax, up on this wall in moments. Anything you do to Weasel will happen to the shield. And if he dies, we'll destroy the sword as well."

Togger stirred uneasily, and the Falcon's eyes narrowed. Had he hit on a threat that might work?

"I don't believe you'd destroy them," she said.

"I don't need them," Edoran replied. "My father, and grandfather, and all my ancestors back to Regalis, ruled just fine without them. I can do the same. You're the one who needs all the symbols you can get."

To his astonishment, Togger laughed.

The Falcon's scowl deepened. "How about this. You come down, yourself, and give them to me. I'll give you Weasel. Then we'll talk about the rest of it. Face-to-face."

"Do I look that stupid?" Edoran's indignation wasn't feigned. If she thought he'd fall for that, he'd been insulted.

"But you'd have Arisa inside," the Falcon said.

Arisa gasped. The Falcon meant to abandon her there. It wasn't as callous as it sounded—Togger's refusal to send her out unless she wanted to go had revealed that the fisherfolk would do her no harm. Still . . .

"No deal," said Edoran. "I'll make you another offer. How about we throw down the sword. You send Weasel to the gate. And when he's safe inside we'll give you the shield. You have my word on that. My word as heir to the throne of Deorthas."

Stall, stall, stall.

"You have to give them to me with your own hands," said the Falcon. "Before witnesses. Or it won't have the effect I need. And you'd still have the offer of regency to bargain with. If I took any of those things by force . . . well, it wouldn't work. The people would hear about it, and sooner or later they'd rebel. But if you gave them to me . . . Yes, I'll make that deal. The sword and shield, given to me freely before witnesses, for Weasel here." Her gaze slid aside.

She really did think he was stupid. Edoran knew that if he left the protection of the fortress, he wouldn't be going back in, no matter what she promised. And while being on the ships when they blew up would be a great way for Prince Edoran to die, it might kill plain Edoran for real. *Stall.*

"What if I refuse?" he asked.

"Then Weasel will start losing bits of himself," the Falcon replied. "Just an earlobe at first. Just enough for him to hurt and bleed, and for you to see I'm serious."

"And you think blackmailing me into giving you the sword and shield, blackmailing me before witnesses, isn't going to spoil your effect?"

The Falcon shrugged and looked away once more. But it wasn't his gaze she was avoiding, Edoran realized. Arisa was staring at her mother, eyes burning in her white, determined face.

"I don't think I'll have to go very far," the Falcon told him. "I think the first spurt of blood will bring you down here."

"But if everyone sees I'm being forced," Edoran argued, "won't it—"

The Falcon drew her knife.

"Wait!" Edoran cried. "Wait a minute. I know you're rotting serious. I'll come down."

"Don't!" Weasel shouted. "That's what she wants. You never do what your enemy wants."

One of the officers clapped a hand over his mouth, muffling further advice.

"He's right, lad," Togger muttered. "Doing what your enemy wants always makes things worse."

"But she's going to do it," Edoran said. "She doesn't care about witnesses."

She didn't care what the fisherfolk saw. Because she didn't intend to leave any witnesses alive. She would storm the fortress as soon as Edoran was safely in her hands. But if he didn't go down, she'd cut Weasel to bits. And then storm the fortress anyway.

He had to get Weasel into the fortress, or he'd die. And if the ships didn't blow before the fortress fell, they'd all die. Surrendering himself wouldn't save the people of Caerfalas, whatever she said. The only thing that might save them was cutting off the pirates' escape route . . . he should have signaled for half an hour, an hour was way too long. But he had to try.

He saw the same realization on the faces of the fisherfolk as he climbed down the ladder. When his feet touched the earth, the sound of hundreds of hoofbeats, galloping closer and closer, rang in his ears. Edoran staggered, almost falling. A sensing. Were the guards finally coming? Or was his desperate need deceiving him, sending his strange perceptions far into the distance, too far for anyone to arrive in time?

If he could stall the Falcon till the ships blew, could he get himself and Weasel back into the fortress under cover of that distraction?

With escape cut off, surely she'd run for the countryside, especially if she had the sword and shield with which to buy her freedom.

Togger had remained on the wall, but Moll stood near the gate with the sword and shield in her hands.

"Lad, I don't like this. I don't think you'll get back in, even if you can keep her talking till the ships blow."

"I know." Edoran hoped the Falcon couldn't read him as well as Moll could. "But she'll cut Weasel to pieces if I don't go out. Then she'll kill him."

"Once she has what she wants, she'll kill you," Moll said. "Sooner or later she'll have to."

"She'll have to kill me first."

Arisa stood before him, knife in hand. Her face was still the color of chalk, but her eyes were alive with grim purpose. "From this moment forward, I'm his bodyguard."

Even the most determined bodyguard could be overcome. At best, Arisa would only buy them a few more moments of time . . . but every moment might count.

"Open the gate," Edoran commanded.

Arisa went out before him, keeping herself between him and the Falcon as they walked across the open ground. Weasel was struggling in the officer's grip. Looking over the crowd behind the Falcon, Edoran saw that the navy sailors wore the same expression he'd seen on the faces of the fisherfolk—if anything, the sailors looked even more dismayed. They would soon be ordered to kill their own people, and they didn't want to. Some of them were slipping back through the crowd, and others, who'd reached the rear, were drifting into the hills, running from a fight they wanted no part of.

So all the decent men on the other side would soon be gone. Wonderful.

They were halfway between the gate and the Falcon when Arisa flung out her arm to stop him. Edoran stopped.

"You can talk from here," Arisa told them both.

The Falcon was staring at her daughter, and her face had gone white. For the first time, Edoran saw a resemblance between them.

"I'm sorry, love," the Falcon said softly. "But this is . . . One day you'll understand."

"I understand now," said Arisa.

The Falcon winced and turned to Edoran. "The sword and shield, Your Highness. Or he dies."

Edoran had no idea how long it would take the swimmers to reach the ships. Were the fuses burning now? Not enough time had passed.

"You're going to regret taking me on a boat," he told the Falcon. "I get seasick. I might even die of it. Some people do."

He'd heard that somewhere, hadn't he?

"Don't worry about it," said the Falcon. "Your Highness won't be so inconvenienced."

Edoran frowned. How could he not get seasick if they escaped in a ship? Then it hit him.

"You're going by land? I don't believe it! There are troops looking for you everywhere!"

"They *were* looking everywhere," the Falcon told him. "Until they learned we'd escaped by sea. Now most of them have been pulled back to assist the navy. So we'll be traveling by land. Master Giles was very helpful in carrying messages to my men."

Were the hoofbeats he'd sensed those of her men's arrival?

"I get sick in a coach, too," Edoran said desperately, "if it travels too fast. I'm not accustomed to riding all day either."

Master Giles pushed his way to the Falcon's side. "That's not true, my lady. He's stalling!"

The Falcon looked at Edoran and nodded. Then, before Edoran had time to realize what she was doing, she grabbed Weasel's ear, drew her knife, and cut off the lobe.

Weasel yelped, and so did Edoran.

"Stop! All right, you can have them!"

He darted around Arisa's frozen form and hurried forward, the sword and shield in his hands. Blood was streaming down Weasel's neck. Even with his eyes fixed on the Falcon and his friend, Edoran was aware that more of the sailors were melting out of the crowd, perhaps a few officers as well. Enough to weaken the Falcon's force too much for her to take the fortress? Probably not.

Arisa was running to catch up to him, but he had reached the Falcon already. He dropped the sword and shield to the ground at her feet. "Take them. They're not worth even a piece of Weasel's ear."

Only hunks of wood and metal, Justice Holis had once said. And Edoran knew it was true.

The crowd had fallen silent.

The Falcon sheathed her knife and picked up first the shield, then the sword. She held the sword as if she knew how to use it.

"Thank you, Your Highness." She turned to the officers beside her. "Let the boy go."

Weasel fought free of their loosening grip and hurtled to stand before Edoran. "Of all the stupid, lamebrained, idiotic stunts!"

He was between Edoran and the Falcon now, and Arisa pushed past the prince to stand with him. Weasel on the right and Arisa on the left. The image of the cards Arisa had laid out floated through his mind: the fool, with the storm protecting him and the hanged man guiding him true.

No matter how powerful the sword and shield were supposed to be, Weasel and Arisa mattered more.

"Of course," the Falcon's quiet voice was clear in the stillness, "I never agreed to let anyone but Weasel go. But thank you for giving me these," she added. "Willingly and freely."

She lifted the sword and shield for all to see.

Edoran could have argued the willing and free part, but suddenly, in a dizzying flash, the truth came clear. How could he have missed it? How many of those statues had Edoran seen over the years? Dozens of different men and women flanking their king . . . holding the *symbols* of their office.

"I do give them to you," he announced. "Of my free will. Because this is my sword." He laid a hand on Arisa's shoulder. "And Weasel is my shield. What you hold are only pieces of iron."

A muffled roar arose, from the sailors behind the Falcon, from the fortress behind Edoran. In that roar he heard dozens of voices babbling, "He's claimed them! The king has claimed them!"

Edoran frowned. He wouldn't be king for years. And he'd always claimed Weasel and Arisa—

Sandeman shoved his way through the crowd to stand before Edoran. Where in the One God's name had he come from? His clothes were rumpled and dirty, and he was sweating despite the cool breeze.

His appearance was so sudden that the Falcon stepped back a pace, her hand tightening on the sword. But the Hidden priest wasn't armed.

"The king has claimed the sword and shield," he said, in a voice that carried to the farthest edge of the crowd. "Now I offer him his crown."

Edoran was wondering how he'd claimed a sword and shield that he'd just handed over to the Falcon, when Sandeman seized his left hand in a strong grip, pulled out a penknife, and slashed a cut across Edoran's palm. Before Edoran even had time to flinch, Sandeman fell to his knees, dragging Edoran down with him, and slammed his cut palm flat on the earth.

The shock reverberated through him like a too-near lightning strike. Like someone had struck a huge bell with a sledgehammer, not to ring it, but to shatter it.

Edoran didn't shatter, but his head was spinning when Sandeman folded his fingers over a handful of bloody mud and pulled him to his feet. Then the priest opened Edoran's fingers, took a pinch of the mud, and drew a gritty line across Edoran's forehead.

It crashed down like an ocean wave, swamping him, drowning him in sensation and knowledge, and he could only snatch at bits as the flood whirled through him. Somewhere in Deorthas a huntsman killed a deer, his shot so close to the beast's heart that it only staggered one step before it crumpled and died. Somewhere a couple was married, the girl eager and proud, the young man far more nervous than she. There was a kitchen, full of the scent of baking bread, where an older woman stirred a bowl, with one granddaughter helping her and another clinging to her skirt. A wheelwright tried to tap a spoke into a wheel, and swore when it snapped. A mill gate opened, sending water over a wheel, and the wheel above it began to turn. Somewhere in the straits, a fishing crew dropped a net full of fish to the deck. A dyer pulled a load of saffron-colored yarn, dripping, from the vat. A small boy dragged a platter of sweet cakes off a counter and burst into tears when the plate fell and shattered.

The images filled Edoran's mind, flowing past and past, washing him away till he couldn't even snatch at them. But slowly one image grew stronger than the others. Somewhere men were fighting a battle, filled with fear and purpose. The strike of a knife over an arm felt as if it cut his own flesh, and Edoran remembered that he had flesh. He could hear the furious shouts, not only in his mind, but with his ears. Edoran focused on physical sensation, held on to the sounds, and dragged himself back into his body, struggling to push that staggering . . . awareness aside.

He opened his eyes. He was on his hands and knees, the mud soaking into his britches. And it hadn't been a trick of his sensing—there was a battle going on around him. He raised his head just in time to see a pirate's knife sweep Arisa's blade aside, and his fist push past her guard to connect solidly with her jaw.

She fell like a dropped rag doll. Edoran started to crawl toward her, but Weasel kicked his wrist. "Stay put! They're after you, not her."

Weasel was in front of him, between him and the pirates, and Sandeman was with him. But other men were running toward them, their footfalls pounding through the earth into his hands.

Edoran lifted his hands and stared, as a wave of shouting guardsmen crashed into the pirate forces around him. The clash of swords, the blood and shouted curses, helped center him in this place and himself, though he still couldn't summon enough sense to be terrified.

He did stagger out and grab Arisa's collar, intending to haul her back to safety, but a strong hand seized his arm and another reached down and took a handful of Arisa's shirt, pulling both of them out of reach of the fighting.

Edoran blinked up into General Diccon's furious face. "What are you doing here?"

"Looking for you, you rotten little . . . Your Highness," the general said through gritted teeth. "We'd have found you weeks ago if that meddler Sandeman hadn't been laying false trails. I should have his hide for that."

"Don't be hasty," said the Hidden priest soothingly. "If I hadn't spent the past few weeks running you around the countryside, I wouldn't have been able to locate you so quickly when I recognized that girl from Caerfalas. Riding a lathered horse far harder than she would have if it wasn't urgent."

"It's still urgent," said Diccon, gazing over the battlefield.

Edoran knew without looking that the Falcon's men were being pushed back toward the beach. But there was a ring of guardsmen now, surrounding him and Weasel and Arisa. He could feel the exact moment the Falcon realized that and decided to cut her losses.

"Into that fortress, Your Highness," the general said. "I've got pirates to capture. Sandeman, see to it." He strode off to take control of the battle.

"Your Highness?" Sandeman gestured to the fortress. Moll had opened the gate and was gesturing for them to come in. "It sounds like a good idea to me."

"It doesn't matter," Edoran said. "We're safe here, as long as the troops stay." His certainty was clear in his voice, and Sandeman looked at him with an expression Edoran couldn't interpret.

"What's it like?"

"Horrible," said Edoran honestly. "I think I'm going to be sick." But he wasn't sure if his queasiness sprang from his own shock, or from the stuff the manufactories of the city were dumping into the river. Just as the burning sensation running up his left shin was actually a forest fire in the woods north of Briston. Fortunately, the wind was pushing the flames toward a snowfield, where they'd soon burn out on their own.

Edoran clenched his teeth and forced his awareness back to . . . not the present, he realized, but this place.

"What did you do to me?" he demanded.

Sandeman's lips twitched. "You're probably the first king since Brent who's had to ask that question. And I can see that if you weren't expecting it . . . This is the crown of earth, Your Highness. You'll get used to it. They all did. And now, if you'll excuse me, I think I can be of some assistance to the wounded. I'm a fair herbalist, you know."

He backed off and vanished. If Edoran hadn't been able to feel the agony of those wounds he'd have murdered the man. Assuming he could find a weapon. And control his reeling mind long enough to use it.

He scrubbed at the dirt on his forehead, hoping that rubbing it off would lessen the uncomfortable sensations that still flashed through him, but it made no difference. He went over to where Weasel sat, with Arisa's head in his lap. She had begun to stir and mutter, and Edoran knew she'd soon recover from the blow to her jaw. The blow to her heart was another matter.

"That," said Weasel critically, "was thoroughly stupid. Never do what your enemies want."

"Why not?" Edoran asked. "I couldn't do what I wanted."

Ron the fisherboy had died today, and with him Edoran's only chance of freedom. He wiped at his forehead once more, the mud rough under his hand.

He saw Weasel's worried gaze, but he was still sensing the battle, the red fire of pain, and the cold emptiness of death. Diccon's men were outnumbered. The only reason they weren't losing was that the Falcon, in possession of the sword and shield, had ordered her men to retreat to their ships.

The ships in whose belly Edoran could feel the glowing worms of lit fuses, slowly burning down.

Diccon was trying to stop her. Diccon's men were dying to stop her from escaping, their lives snuffing out like candle flames, but achingly more precious, and never to be relit in this world.

Edoran made his first decision as king. It felt just as wretched as he'd known it would.

The guardsmen tried to argue when he insisted on being taken to the general, but when he commanded it, to his own astonishment they gave way and escorted him there.

Diccon had found a low hillock from which he could see the whole sweep of fortress, village, and beach. His lips, as he assessed the progress of the uneven fight, were set in a grim line.

"What are you doing here?" he snapped before Edoran could speak. "I told you to get into that fortress. The only reason she's retreating is that she thinks you're inside those walls!"

This wasn't the moment to argue about the general's right to give him orders.

"Let her go," Edoran said. "Stop fighting and let her retreat."

A muscle tightened in the general's jaw. "I almost wish I could, but if those pirates escape . . . We've spent months trying to track them down. I can't let them get away, to start it all over again."

"They won't get far," said Edoran wearily. Did he have the strength, the mental focus, to give the general a coherent explanation of the fuses in those ships' powder stores, and how they came to be lit? He certainly couldn't explain how he knew the swimmers had succeeded in their task. The spark of those burning fuses flared more clearly in his mind than the general's face in bright sunlight.

"Let her go," he repeated. "She's going to make it anyway. Trying to stop her just wastes your men's lives."

The general's face was rigid with resistance; then his shoulders slumped. "You're right. I just . . . You're right. Your Highness."

He turned to give the order to one of his officers, and Edoran walked away. By the time he'd hiked back to Weasel and Arisa, the battle was ending. The longboats had been launched, and the pirates were on the way back to their ships, with only a few hopeful guardsmen firing shots from the beach.

Arisa was still flat on her back, but she had one hand pressed against her head, and her eyelids were crimped tight with pain.

Weasel's face was tight with frustration. "You can't let her get away! She'll try again, and this time she's got the sword and shield!"

"No, she doesn't." That truth gave Edoran nothing but peace. "I just hope you're willing to repeat that statement when Arisa's really awake."

Edoran had made the decision to stop the Falcon himself—but he'd be happy to share some of the blame.

"I am awake," said Arisa hazily. "Repeat what?"

"Nothing," said Edoran, glaring Weasel to silence. It was bad enough that he'd condemned her mother to death—she didn't need to watch it.

But Arisa knew him too well. She opened her eyes and looked around, over the field where the battle had taken place, over the empty beach, out to the bay where the pirate ships were unfurling their sails.

She screamed, a shrill, tearing sound that made Edoran flinch. She fought free of Weasel's restraining hands, clawing his face when he tried to stop her. She ran down the road almost a hundred yards before she realized that there was nothing she could do, no way she could stop it. She was no longer screaming, but stood staring, with both hands pressed over her mouth. Shudders ran through her body, shaking her so hard that even at that distance Edoran could see them.

Weasel hurried after her, and Edoran followed more slowly. He had almost reached them when the ships blew up, wood and flame boiling into the sky.

A moan forced its way past Arisa's hands. She slipped through Weasel's clutch and huddled on the sand, sobbing. Her anguish and shame resonated through Edoran, worse, far worse, than the pain of his gathering headache.

Weasel sank down beside her and put his arms around her, but his eyes met Edoran's steadily.

"You did the right thing. She'd never have stopped, and sooner or later hundreds would have died. You did right."

"I know," said Edoran. But why did it have to hurt so much? Hurt Arisa, who didn't deserve it. And hurt him, too, with the death of his dreams.

But perhaps Ron the fisherboy wasn't completely dead, for he sat down on the dirt beside Arisa and wrapped his arms around her too. And that was something Prince Edoran could never have done.

CHAPTER 13

THE LADY

The Lady: wealth, fertility, peace.

To Prince Edoran's astonishment, Ron the fisherboy lingered on—perhaps because when he returned to the city he took a piece of Caerfalas with him.

"It's only a common sweater." Moll had looked nervous, saying her farewells in front of the general who commanded Deorthas' army. "But we knitted in your name, as well as the pattern for Caerfalas. It's got Togger and my family pattern, too, with a band to show that you're . . . adopted, in a sense. Once we realized you were worth adopting into the family, you see."

Laughter crinkled the corners of her eyes. She was nervous of General Diccon, but not of him. And she said nothing about the name in the sweater being "Ron" and not Edoran, though she added, "I suppose, being a prince and all, you'll not have much need of it."

Edoran, who was still wearing his fishing clothes, stripped off the guest sweater and pulled on the one she held out to him. He could tell by looking at the general's hunched shoulders that his sweater cut the cold spring wind better than Diccon's fancy jacket.

He also knew how long it took to knit one of these, and how little free time Moll had had in the past few days. She must have started it shortly after the fishing fleet set sail, and Edoran had to swallow down the lump in his throat in order to reply.

"This prince has developed a taste for sailing. I'll wear it every time I set foot on a deck, and it will keep me warm and safe."

He'd recognized some of the old gods' sigils that were knitted in, though there were others he didn't recognize, and perhaps those were for . . . remembering? Being true to yourself? Maybe it was just the affection that came with the gift, but even as the familiar luxury of palace life closed in around him, Edoran found that Ron the fisherboy, far from dying, seemed to be showing up more and more often.

It was certainly Ron who was scratching his bare feet as he sat on Weasel's bed, chatting with his friend, on the afternoon that Sandeman came to make his farewells.

Edoran sat up in alarm when he saw the man's worn traveling clothes. "You're leaving? So soon? How will I . . . Ah, have you had trouble with the courtiers?"

He'd introduced the Hidden priest to his court simply as "my welcome guest," and there'd been so much else for them to gossip about that Edoran had thought the courtiers mostly ignored him.

"It's not that," said Sandeman. "Everything here is fine. You'll do perfectly well without me—although you'll be happier if you try for some control, instead of scratching your feet raw."

Edoran blushed. He knew that the itching in the soles of his feet was really the beginning of a crop blight, in the winter wheat fields south of Westerfen. He'd already sent a message warning the farmers about the threat to their crops, but the wheat had to reach a certain stage in its development before it could be dusted with the powder that would kill the blight. Both the university chemists who'd created the powder and the farmers who'd used it in previous years had told him that. So until the wheat grew to the right height, he had to either suffer the itch or exercise the mental controls Sandeman had taught him.

That was becoming easier, and Edoran knew that eventually it would be something he could do without even thinking about it—but for now, unless he concentrated on handling the sensation, his feet itched. And the itch was beginning to spread up his ankles.

He focused now, finding the source of the irritation, which was not in his feet but in his sensing, and firmly shutting it . . . not down, but away. Locked in a mental box, until he had need to check on the situation.

The itching vanished, and Edoran pulled on his stockings, feeling that was more dignified for a serious discussion.

"If everything's fine, why are you going?" he asked.

"In a sense, it's because everything's fine," Sandeman said. "If I'm about to become the head of a legal church—legal for the first time in centuries!—I'd better start organizing. It feels odd, after all this time, to step into the light."

Some of that light was already in his face, and Edoran sighed. "I suppose you must."

That would teach him to pick men of true faith for his advisers.

"You know," said Weasel critically, "you could have wiped that mud on his forehead when you first met and saved us a lot of trouble. Or better yet, when you and I first met! It might have . . . A lot of things might have been different."

They all knew what he meant. Miraculously, Arisa didn't blame any of them for her mother's death, not even Edoran, but she still grieved. It was hard to watch, though Edoran's sensing told him she would heal eventually—and that the scars left by her mother's dishonor would be deeper than those left by her death. Those same scars would keep Arisa from ever following her mother's path. But it was just as well she wasn't encountering any of the courtiers these days.

She spent most of her time with Yallin, the Hidden's seamstress-spy, and the old woman's company seemed to be doing her some good.

And Yallin showed no sign of going anywhere, so Edoran would have someone to go to when his unfamiliar gift baffled him.

But Sandeman was finally answering Weasel's complaint.

"I couldn't do anything when we first met, my boy, or even when Edoran and I first met, because at that time none of you had become what you needed to be."

Weasel frowned. "I don't understand."

Sandeman had already explained it to Edoran, but Edoran had understood the heart of the matter since that moment on the beach.

Now the Hidden priest sighed. "It was Deor's death that forged the crown of earth, the link between any of his descendants who would become king and the whole land of Deorthas. The teachers of that time feared the link would grow weaker as the generations passed."

"It didn't," said Edoran dryly.

Sandeman laughed, curse him. "I think that although it took Deor's death to create the link, somehow those old teachers managed to fuel it with the withe that exists in every living thing, to keep its power always fresh. Though some of the other teachers disagree about the power's source. We're still arguing about it."

His eyes twinkled, and Weasel snorted.

"But however it was fueled, the crown was forged," Sandeman went on. "And King Brent, who first experienced it, was even more shocked and baffled than you were."

"I doubt that," Edoran said.

"He was angry about it," Sandeman told them. "According to our histories he hated the gods for what he saw as a curse, and for his father's death. So the gods granted him one final gift."

"The sword and shield," Weasel put in. "Which weren't actually a sword and shield, but his two chief advisers."

Sandeman shook his head. "Not exactly. What the gods gave Brent, and his heirs, was the ability to recognize the right people to fill those jobs."

That part of the story had traveled across the realm with a speed that made Edoran suspect magic—certainly no horse could have moved that fast. In the countryside, a startling number of people remembered enough to understand what it meant when the king claimed the sword and shield. The populace of the city neither understood nor cared, but that was a problem for the future. Edoran had enough troubles right now.

"Neither the sword nor the shield is infallible," Sandeman

went on. "Their advice isn't divinely inspired. Sometimes they'll disagree with each other. And kings have been known to go against their advice as well. Look at the woman Regalis' father married."

"You mean even with Weasel and Arisa's advice, I can still screw up?" Edoran asked. "Wonderful."

Weasel looked interested. "So Regalis really was someone else's son? You can prove it?"

Sandeman grimaced. "I don't have documents, or anything like that, but it was proven to our teachers' satisfaction, because . . . You have to understand, more than a thousand years had passed since Deor and Brend, and certain traditions had been developed by both our faith and the royal family. The most important was that our teachers had realized that the moment when an heir claimed the sword and shield marked the moment he was ready to receive the crown of earth. It wasn't any set age, though I think all of them were at least in their teens when they recognized their sword and shield. And that didn't always happen at the same time, either. Sometimes an heir would claim one or the other, but wait for years till he could . . . well, complete the set. In those first centuries, the noble families would fight, sometimes even kill, to get their kinsmen into a position where a prince might choose them."

"Like shareholders sending their daughters to court," said Edoran, growing interested himself. He hadn't heard this part of it before.

"Like that in some ways, but a lot less civilized," Sandeman told him. "Those were violent times. The idea of one king ruling the whole realm was still a new one—and not entirely popular. Anyway, over time the teachers decided that only when an heir had claimed both sword and shield would he be given the crown. Sometimes that didn't happen till after he'd inherited the throne, so it soon became a private ceremony.

"The country folk all remembered what it meant, but with the rise of the narrow god's church—which performed the official ceremony when a new king took the throne—the city people soon forgot that another ceremony even existed. And the kings themselves developed . . . a family tradition, call it. They'd tell their sons about the crown of earth, but they wouldn't tell them what they had to do to get it. The claiming of the sword and shield, which sooner or later all descendants of Brend's blood would accomplish, *was* considered the final confirmation that this was an heir of the true blood."

"And Regalis never claimed the sword and shield?" Edoran asked. "That's how you knew he wasn't the king's son?"

"Oh, he claimed the sword and shield, loudly and repeatedly," Sandeman told them. "But he never claimed the *people* the sword and shield represented."

"I'm surprised some courtier didn't tip him off to the truth, in exchange for being chosen," Weasel said cynically. "Or the servants. Surely some of them came from the country."

"I'm not surprised," said Edoran. "Servants and courtiers . . . they're not really . . ."

"Regalis surrounded himself with people who thought like

he did," Sandeman said. "And the private ceremony . . . Perhaps it was because when the heirs were given the crown they tended to vomit, or faint, or fall over"—he nodded to Edoran—"but the private ceremony had become very private. A lot of nobles didn't know what claiming the sword and shield entailed, and some didn't believe the gods' gifts were real, even though their king demonstrated them all the time. They thought he had 'good sources of information' or some such thing."

"So with Regalis, the line of Deor's descendants was broken," Edoran said. "And none of his heirs knew the truth."

"And the old faith had been outlawed," said Sandeman. "In part for pointing out to those who did remember that this king was not of the true blood."

"So in a way," said Weasel, "you're responsible for all the problems between the city and the countryside yourselves."

Sandeman scowled. "That's a vast oversimplification! And Regalis *was* a false king. It was our duty to . . ."

Weasel's overly innocent expression gave the game away, and Sandeman stopped, the scowl fading. "All right, you got me going. Perhaps some of it was our fault, though mostly it was the drought, taxes, and Regalis' own preference for . . . for regarding the country as something that existed only to produce food for the important people. The important people, in his mind, being nobles and the craftsmen who produced their luxuries. So it all fell apart. And there was no heir of Deor's blood to put it back together . . . until now."

Edoran, feeling that heavy burden descending on his shoulders, grimaced. "So my father wasn't descended from Deor?" His father had suspected that himself, writing about it in his journals, but Edoran had always hoped . . .

"No. He was a good man," Sandeman said. "He might have been a good king. Several of Regalis' descendants were both those things. But Deor's blood came to you through your mother's family."

"You told me that your father was doing genealogical research when he met her, didn't you?" Weasel asked.

Edoran nodded. He barely remembered his mother, but his father . . .

"He was a good man," the Hidden priest repeated. "He did his best. Let the rest of it go."

"So when did you realize you had a true heir again?" Weasel asked.

"When he claimed the sword and shield," Sandeman replied. "Right in the middle of what was about to turn into a pitched battle, between a mob of pirates and a group of guardsmen they outnumbered three to one! I'm not sure," he added thoughtfully, "but I think that was the worst moment for a claiming in the entire history of the realm."

"Had I been warned," said Edoran with dignity, "I might have done it sooner. Under better circumstances. And Arisa's mother might still be alive."

Or executed for treason. Or in prison. Or still in a position of power, plotting to murder her way to the throne.

"Don't you understand yet?" Sandeman's voice was oddly

gentle. "You couldn't have chosen them earlier. They hadn't yet become what they needed to be, in order to be the sword and shield you needed. When you first met him, Weasel was a small-souled pickpocket—"

"Ex-pickpocket," Weasel inserted.

"—whose primary goal in life was to become a forger. And Arisa," the priest went on, "was in a fair way to becoming the kind of fanatic that no sane person wants in charge of their military. As for you, ah . . ."

"As for me, I was the last person anyone would want on a throne," said Edoran. "And I wouldn't have recognized the true sword and shield if they'd bitten me on the ankle."

He realized why that particular phrase had occurred to him, and scratched his ankle vigorously before banishing the sensation once more.

"None of this was guaranteed in the beginning," Sandeman finished. "All we could do was keep an eye on the three of you and pray you'd grow into what you had to be . . . without getting yourselves killed in the process. You made a pretty fair attempt at that," he added.

"I was trying to keep everyone alive!" Weasel said indignantly.

Edoran regarded the Hidden priest thoughtfully. "I made a mess of things, didn't I?"

"It was messy," Sandeman admitted. "But you didn't do too badly. All in all, I think you managed pretty well."

Edoran snorted. "All I did was get rescued. Three times. I never rescued myself, not even once!"

"Maybe not," Sandeman said. "But you did save Caerfalas' boats. And whoever the pirates would have preyed on in the future. And you saved the whole realm from the Falcon's schemes. That, my boy, is what kings are supposed to do. They have minions to rescue them, should they ever be so foolish as to need it. Again. Which would be *really* foolish."

Because he wouldn't be around to do it. "I won't," Edoran said. "Well, I'll try not to. Before you go . . . would you lay the cards for me? For my future?"

If anything was about to go wrong, it would be nice to have warning.

Sandeman shook his head. "You can do that for yourself, should you need to," he said. "Or Arisa can do it for you. But you already know what you'd see."

He left then, closing the door behind him.

"That was cryptic," Weasel grumbled.

But Edoran did know what he'd see if he laid the cards: the fool, with the storm to his left and the hanged man to his right.

He didn't know everything. He didn't know how people would react to the worship of the old gods being legal once more. He didn't know what Weasel would do or say in the next minute.

But he knew that he needed to reroute the city sewers so they no longer emptied into the river; the bay was almost a desert already, empty not only of fish but of any kind of sea life. That odd fellow at the university, whom everyone ridiculed because he was obsessed with finding a way to turn sewage into clean fertilizer, wouldn't be laughed at so much when he received full crown funding.

Yes, Edoran would need the scientists. He'd need the cooperation of the city workers, who'd embraced the church of the One God, as well . . . though something needed to be done about their working conditions.

The thought of facing down some angry manufactory owner made Edoran cringe, but that was the king's job. And both Weasel and Arisa would be with him when he did it. With Weasel and Arisa at his side, anything was possible. Anything.